THE
JOURNEY

THE JOURNEY

Indira Ganesan

ALFRED A. KNOPF

New York

1990

THIS IS A BORZOI BOOK
PUBLISHED BY ALFRED A. KNOPF, INC.

Library of Congress Cataloging-in-Publication Data

Ganesan, Indira.
    The journey.
    I. Title.
PS3557.A495J68   1990   813'.54   88-45763
ISBN 0-394-56838-9

Manufactured in the United States of America

FIRST EDITION

To my parents and my brother

When I wak'd, I cried to dream again.

—*The Tempest (III, ii)*

Acknowledgments

The author is grateful to the Fine Arts Work Center in Provincetown and the MacDowell Colony for support during the writing of this book.

Material on page 158 was taken from *Ten-Thousand Dreams Interpreted* by Gustavas Miller (New York: Rand McNally).

Special thanks go to Kathy Shorr, Maureen Clyne, Cathleen Micheaels, Lee Briccetti, and Vicky Tomayko for their encouragement and spirit.

One

The women of her mother's village say that if one twin dies by water, the other will die by fire. Renu's cousin Rajesh died on a train. During the crossing from Madhupur to Chombatore, a storm swelled and rode in from the coast, stripping leaves off drenched branches, tangling long-armed bushes and shrubs, uprooting entire palms. The bridge swung back and forth, the rice paddies flooded, and the train, soot-covered and mud-splattered, trembled its way forward, shuddered, and slipped off the tracks into the water below. Her cousin, the Gogol diving from his pocket, his ugly slippers crushed, must have spun like a Catherine wheel in the air, tumbling, his glasses flying as the train fell. It took two days for the news to reach the family in America, two days for them to untwist his body from that unholy and anonymous death. Renu's mother wept and kept her away from the stove all day.

They had always said Rajesh was her twin. Renu's mother and her aunt discovered they'd conceived the same day, and watched over each other's pregnancies. They would untuck their saris and stand naked in front of the mirror, examining their round bellies, comparing the fullness, the smoothness. When their time came on the same day, they kissed each other and held hands during the deliveries. "Rajesh and you were identically wrinkled," said Renu's mother.

When the news arrived, only Renu and her mother were at home. Everyone shouted on the phone. Renu's aunt Chitra said one word and began to weep. Aunt Bala took the receiver from her to bellow, "It's all so horrible." Grandfather Das asked about the weather in the U.S., and no one knew what to say. As Renu watched her mother on the phone, she knew preparations were being made for a flight out of New York. Soon they'd be back, back in the insufferable heat, back in the lazy ripple of an afternoon breeze, back on the streets which smelled of dung and dirt. They would light a fire, they would cast her cousin's body on a pile of sticks, a momentary prince atop a pyramid. But Renu has already left. She's in the gardens, in the dusty paths between the banyan groves, the cool sleeping mats, the netted beds, the circling ceiling fans of their grandfather's house.

Renu's grandfather's house was named "Nirmila Nivasam" after her great-grandfather's wife, a woman who died on a pilgrimage to Benares. Her grandfather, too, wished to die on holy land, and the minute his throat scratched in an unfamiliar way or his head throbbed in a rhythm he couldn't identify, he would demand to be placed on a boat to sanctified land. For years, Bala ignored him, administering balms and medicines. The summer Renu turned ten, though, Grandfather caught a sickness that would not go away, and some actually spoke of taking him to Benares. Bala said he wasn't well enough to travel and persuaded everyone to visit as usual. When Renu's holidays came up, the only other guests at the house were a distant aunt with her baby, her cousin Anu, and Rajesh. She could hardly wait to see Rajesh, having missed him at the last family reunion during Diwali; his parents had taken him to Delhi and he'd promised to bring home an accent.

He was waiting at the station, skinnier than ever. He looked like a starved stray cat, hunching his shoulders, pushing back his broken glasses. Renu taught him an Orissan song she'd learned, and he taught her the words of a new pop tune. *Bye, Bye, Miss American Pie* they sang in the taxi.

Grandfather Das always insisted they pack their schoolbooks with them whenever they visited, "to review for the new term." It never did any good to explain that grade school wasn't made up of accumulated knowledge, that each year was sharply separated. The weight of a previous term dragged Renu's bags to the ground. After their first meal, he summoned the twins to his sickroom and asked them to name the principal river systems in India, the important dates in the French Revolution. Jumna, Godavari, Krishna, Ganga, Renu recited slowly while Rajesh sped through the formations and dissolutions of assemblies and the major beheadings. Their grandfather listened with his eyes closed, frowned at their mistakes, and abruptly dismissed them. They left him as he let go of great coughs.

The summer seemed endless, and the stillness of the long, hot days was broken only by their grandfather's coughs; even that had an ordered meter of its own. But everything changed at night. It wasn't only the dark that descended uneasily but the strangeness. Out came the bats, the snakes, the creatures whose names Renu didn't know, but whose forms she imagined into horrible shapes, unfathomable eyes. Nirmila's ghost was said to visit the garden nightly; she was seen gliding in and out of the trees, the sound of her bangles and anklets distinctly jangling. Sometimes there would be snatches of music, of bells and light drums, and the unmistakable noise of dancers coming from the dark depths of the trees. The aunts gathered on the porch in the evenings and talked of devils and demons who lingered around the earth. They spoke of Kali-worshipers, mad women with matted hair and skull necklaces, possessed by the powerful goddess. The twins knew that no matter how much they were interested in the stories, they could not ask questions; even to say the name of the goddess was to curse themselves.

The privy was located in the back of the garden, and an older cousin or aunt used to walk Renu there at night, carrying a flashlight. Renu hated it when Anu walked with her, holding her hand firmly in her own sweaty one. Anu was the Toad Cousin, with a small, squat head and bulging eyes, the ugliest girl in town. She studied anthropology at school and recited aloud from her *Tribal Cults of the Western Ghats* late into the night. She told stories Renu didn't want to hear, stories Renu recounted to Rajesh, adding gory details at will. If a monster had two heads, Renu would give it six and tremble at her own invention.

The summer in daylight blazed gloriously. Even Anu couldn't stop their happiness. That, though, was checked by the Sanskrit master. He was their grandfather's idea, but they knew Anu must have had a sneaky hand in it. One day the twins tried to climb coconut trees in imitation of the man who eased up and down the burlap trunks to knock down fruit. Grandfather saw them straddling a tree, thought they were in need of civilizing, and hired Mr. Ramdas.

There was nothing the twins dreaded more than the sound of Mr. Ramdas's umbrella clacking on the cobbled street. His step was light, quickening as he approached the porch, a swift figure in a spotless dhoti with a pinched-in pockmarked face.

He was bursting with brains. He permitted only slates, refusing them paper. They each had their own thin chalk pencils which broke as easily as sandstone.

From two to four, when the day was brilliant and inviting, they sat straight-backed and cross-legged on the porch. They'd start off with the alphabet and then go through vocabulary and declensions while Mr. Ramdas offered interruptions, elaborating clausal dilemmas and refining pronunciation. As the twins wrote their lessons, Mr. Ramdas talked god. He spoke of the creation of the world, the creation of death to balance good and evil in the newly created world, the composition of the strands of matter, which are good, evil, and passion. He warned them of the anger of the gods when balances were disturbed, the celestial wrath that caused the earth to split open, fire to consume everything in sight and spit out ash, draping the world in darkness. That such terrors could run out of his mouth so rapidly without his face losing its placid expression filled them with awe.

Comic books provided solace after their lessons. On the cool floor of the storeroom, next to sacks of rice and flour, bins of dried lemons and peppers, Renu and Rajesh spread their comics and read as lizards darted noiselessly across the walls. Rajesh read with his chin cupped in one hand, thin bangs falling over his eyes. Even at ten his hair was falling out, a sign Bala said marked him for the gods. Renu's hair was thick and nothing she did, rubbing bitter roots onto the scalp or merely tugging at it, made it any thinner.

In the comic books, they found a wider range of evil and its manifestations, superbeings who turned cities into powder, sucked away oceans, held back comets and meteors in a breath. This world's laws were defined by Green Lantern's Code and the Justice League. In their games, Anu, Grandfather, and Mr. Ramdas were adversaries as fierce as Black Widow, Magneto, and Doctor Doom.

Eventually came the day when Mr. Ramdas had to visit relatives in another town and classes were canceled. When their aunt told the twins the news, they looked at the ground as if seeking irregular verbs in the grass, but when she told them there would be no work to make up in the master's absence, they could no longer contain their joy. They raced around the courtyard in mad circles, shouting "pow!" and "zowie!"

Archery was their passion those days. Grandfather Das himself had taught them to bend bows from skinny mango branches. They tied the ends with string and peeled long sticks for arrows. There was nothing like the smell of young green branches, a tantalizing moment of expectation, like the first anticipated bite into dark, purple sugarcane.

They chased the monkeys off the roof as they clambered up. The mango and sapota trees trailed their leaves languorously over the red tiles and whitewashed walls. The curved arrows spiraled onto the roof of the porch below while the straight ones, which they named, clattered on the tiles in front of the house. The twins began to compete and drew arrows at the same time.

Renu knew she heard a *thump* or a *thwack*, some unnatural sound. One of the arrows had found a mark. It was a tree trunk, perhaps, or a gold-brown coconut husk, but even at that distance, even through the clump of trees, they saw the fall, the swift, graceless descent of something unknown.

Hurriedly, they made their way down the house, across the yard. There, at the far end of the courtyard, at the foot of the holy jasmine tree, on top of a few crushed flowers, lay a monkey. A young monkey, hunched on its knees with its rear up in the air, much like their baby cousin in sleep.

"It's dead," said Rajesh.

"No, it's just asleep," said Renu.

"It's dead."

"It's just hurt."

"It's dead."

"It's dead," repeated Renu, for so it was.

They were dazed with horror. How could one arrow have killed a monkey, an arrow without a point, an arrow with only a name? What was to be done with it? Should they bury it or merely toss it on the refuse pile like a dead rat? They could not find the arrow anywhere.

"What's happened here?"

Chandran, the gardener, had come upon them so silently they were startled.

"It's dead," blurted out Rajesh.

Chandran clucked his tongue sympathetically and shook his head. Taking a stick, he gently turned the monkey over but found no wound.

"How did it happen?"

Renu and Rajesh were silent.

"It's not hurt—did it just fall?"

"Yes," said Rajesh as Renu vigorously nodded.

And suddenly, incredibly, Chandran's face began to change. His eyes widened and his mouth struggled to smile and form an O at the same time. He began to tremble. He clapped his hands together and shouted for their aunt.

Bala huffed over, her large body heaving under twelve yards of sari. Chandran told her that the monkey had fallen by itself, that the children had discovered it, that it fell near the holy jasmine tree.

"It's Hanuman, it's the god himself!" shouted Chandran.

And to the twins' amazement, Bala's face began to change as well. She underwent the same transformation Chandran had, and the two of them stood shaking and chanting, their hands clasped in devotion.

Hanuman! Hanuman the monkey god, big, strong Hanuman who could carry ten people on each shoulder, whose tail lit up with fire to raze an entire city, who was once sent to fetch a certain herb from a mountainside and brought back the entire mountain—was this Hanuman whom they'd killed? Bala ran to tell Grandfather Das, saying that Hanuman must have meant the young monkey as a sign, and who needed Benares when the god himself had come to restore his health? Renu and Rajesh stood as still as stone, struck by their spontaneous lie. They had killed an emissary of the gods.

Word got around that Hanuman had visited Nirmila Nivasam, that the god had enjoyed some fruit from their garden. "For who has better mangoes than us?" reasoned Aunt Bala. A stream of people came by to see the body, to visit the holy ground, to touch the walls of the house. Bala was enraged and ordered Chandran to lock the gate, but that didn't stop anyone. They, the curious, the enraptured, hung onto the gate to peer through the bars while Chandran repeated the story as if it were he who had discovered the monkey. And in that crowd of worship, in that frenzy of belief, someone suggested a shrine be built, that the occasion not be let by so casually.

Renu and Rajesh felt sick at dinner. Bala recalled the time she had had a vision of god when young. "I myself have seen Krishna in the banyan grove. He was standing right there with his little finger cocked and his peacock feather askew. And you know," she said, swallowing a mouthful, "I have never slept well since." Renu knew then that she too would be plagued with insomnia. Grandfather Das insisted on eating with them, declaring he felt better already. "The last time there was a visit from a god in town was when Sri Venkateswara walked through the old market, where Lolly's Emporium is now. That was long before Independence," he said, his voice raspy. Bala finally noticed the twins' flushed faces and sent them to bed. "Too much excitement," she said.

"Why can't we tell them?" asked Renu.

"We killed him, we can't tell anyone," said Rajesh.

They consulted Anu's textbooks and learned that an animal's unnatural death usually foretold disaster. In some tribes, people were stoned for killing an ox or a goat.

"They won't throw rocks at us—that's stupid," said Rajesh.

"We should run away," said Renu.

Renu slept fitfully that night. She heard her grandfather and her aunt arguing over whether he should be allowed to smoke. She dreamed of being chased by monkeys. She saw Brahma opening and closing his mouth as cities slipped on and off his tongue. She dreamed of being whirled away into nothingness, that awful place Mr. Ramdas spoke of. She realized she was without hope. Renu shared a room with Anu, whose very snores sounded ominous.

A collection was taken and builders were contracted. The masons came over to discuss the type of stone to be used for the shrine, the color, the texture. It was to be a small one, on the corner of Deena and Victoria, across the street from Roy's sweetshop. Their grandfather believed that walking would help his illness, and stopped to inspect the work every day. The twins accompanied him on these junkets, urging him to slow his pace, rest a while, all of which he ignored. As soon as they neared the construction, Renu and Rajesh would mutter excuses to their grandfather and run on to Roy's store. There they would sit on the ice cooler, sucking at orange Fantas, reading comics until Grandfather Das was ready to leave. But not even the Phantom offered them any sanctuary. That purple-skinned mystic seemed to point a finger at them as he admonished his readers to turn in thieves, government spies, liars of all kinds.

In the days that followed, Renu was filled with a desperate sense of foreboding. She and Rajesh had tampered with a divine scheme and they would be punished. At first, they worried about their grandfather, who was determined to recover as rapidly as possible. One morning Renu heard him bathing without waiting for someone to heat the water. She banged on the door, terrified he would collapse to the floor. "Go back to bed! The gods are looking after me," he thundered. It seemed they might be, for he did look better. Maybe they hadn't really hit the monkey, maybe it just had had a heart attack. But they had seen it fall, they stepped in by not telling the truth, they upset the balance, they were causing the world to totter dangerously. Renu sighed. Nothing could be hidden from the gods. What everyone took to be a good sign she knew signalled doom.

The builders were fast, and in a week the town had a new shrine. Everyone was going to be present at the shrine-initiating ceremony. The house filled with the sound of rustling silk as the whole family prepared for the event. Renu had to have her hair washed and anointed with oil, stand still as her aunt stretched and pulled it into braids with new ribbons.

"Why are you squirming? We're going to Binder's after the prayers."

But Renu knew she'd never make it to Binder's Hotel, where they served real American sundaes. Whatever punishment the gods meant to deliver would arrive at the ceremony. The twins were miserable on their way into town.

Renu tried to imagine the horror that awaited them. The earth might break open, swallowing the shrine and them with it, or maybe there would be an awful moment of communal truth, when all fingers would point to them in anger and outrage. Maybe there would be something even worse. She tried to think of something worse as she prepared herself for death.

A small crowd had already gathered in front of the shrine. A flat-bellied priest was accepting flowers and fruits for sanctifying. Renu and Rajesh tried to linger behind, but Bala grabbed them firmly by the shoulders.

"Think of it, you're heroes in a way. Don't be shy," she said, her grip, falcon talons.

Renu wondered if they were destined for reductive reincarnation, if they'd be turned into moths or spiders. Maybe it would be only Rajesh who'd get into trouble, since he had lied first, but since they were twins, Renu thought in a rush of loyalty and melodrama, she shared in his fate.

The priest began the prayers. A baby started to cry and her mother shushed her. Renu wondered if they'd be struck mad. "Rama-Rama-Rama," chanted Chandran at the edge of the crowd, nearly drowning out the priest's words. Maybe they'd be turned into stone. Rajesh stuck his hands in his pockets and refused to look at her.

Hungry village boys stood in a group, waiting for the coconuts to be broken so they could steal the pieces home. A woman brought her baby, green with colic, to be cured. A blind woman touched her eyes in silent supplication. Two armless men worked their way to the front of the crowd where the priest rubbed red powder onto their foreheads. Renu realized the enormity of her crime. The earth whirled.

"She's dead, she's dead," shouted Rajesh as she hit the ground.

. . .

Renu woke to white mist. Bala parted the mosquito netting and handed her a glass of juice. "It must have been the heat and the crowd," she said.

Renu and Rajesh spoke of the events a good deal that night. They were mystified. They did not understand why the gods had overlooked them. The shrine had not fallen apart, Grandfather was still in good health. Despite everything, they could not whisper away the sense of imminent doom, the notion that everything was waiting to explode, that the gods were only biding their time.

The shrine remained popular for a while. Anu said that people were god-mad, that they always looked for a new place to worship. The following summer, Renu's family moved to America. She and Rajesh wrote thick or thin letters, depending on their moods. Once he wrote that few people remembered the shrine, and seemed to shrug the whole thing off. "We were just spooked kids," he wrote. They never referred to the incident again.

It had remained with Renu all these years, though. Whenever she slipped into the American way of life, when she stopped wearing the red *tikká* on her forehead, when she stopped going to temple, she could not free herself of the idea that the gods were still hunting her, that they were waiting to seek retribution.

Outside, the rain sounded as if it were wearing away the roof, making pools in the lawn, sinking the house. Tomorrow she would go through the photographs, the letters—it was enough now to summon up his face. But already the memory was dim, one minute indelible in her mind, the next minute gone. They would probably not let her see the cremation, believing the sight to be more than unmarried girls could stand. But she was determined to attend to the rites; she would say good-bye to her cousin, her childhood companion, her twin. She would brave those flames.

In the kitchen, she heard her mother drop a plate. They would eat sparely tonight.

Two

The Parsis of Bombay consider the body so functional, they offer their dead to the birds. On the morning the Krishnans arrived at Bombay Airport, a vulture headed for a funerary feast collided with the propeller of an airborne plane. A woman clutching black feathers in her hands told them this: "You can still smell death in the air," she said. Rukmani Krishnan hurried her two daughters away. This was no time to be told of a bad omen, she thought, keeping an eye out for every bad luck sneeze and gesture. Renu slipped a feather in her pocket.

They took the connecting flight to Madras, and then boarded a boat to take them to the island. They passed what looked like a bridge under construction. Ten years ago, a Nigerian artist had received a land grant to build an ash mound on Pi. He created a hill of shredded paper, glue, ash, and added bits of wooden and plastic castoffs he'd found on the beach. It glittered like a bejeweled stupa, a Christmas tree, a baked Alaska. But the rains came two days after the project's completion and reduced it to a pulpy mess. Tourists and islanders scavenged the remains and to this day many houses on Pi have pieces of art affixed to their doors. Now the same artist was building a bridge to connect the mainland to Pi.

When they stepped off the boat, Rukmani had counted twenty-three bad omens and Renu could still smell death in the air. In Grandfather Das's car, a monstrous red Ambassador whose seats smelled of cardamom, they drove up the damp road to Madhupur. Past the beach, the foliage seemed to shout at them, flowers demanding attention. Here were lush grasses, flowers shot with magenta, hanging bushes of jasmine, and red-throated hibiscus. As always, the island seemed overwhelming, as if it could swallow up everything in its brilliance.

When a group of lost white explorers found shelter on the island in 1726, they thought they'd stumbled onto Paradise. The captain, a man smitten with Shakespeare, claimed it for Holland and named it Prospero's Island; ever since, it has been known as P.I. or Pi. To the surprise of the Dutch, who thought the island uninhabited, Pi contained prosperous cities built on citadels, the largest of which was Madhupur. Kings and queens, resplendent in jewels and silks, ate from golden plates while their darker-hued workers toiled on repairing heavily trafficked roads. In less than a century, however, with the arrival of the French and the English, the imperialist conquest was complete, and the power transferred from the rajahs to the Europeans, where it remained under colonial rule until 1947. That year, depleted of nearly all its natural resources and having undergone a cultural identity crisis made all the more severe because of the island's small size, Pi was grudgingly granted independence. Imagine a chunk of India that is not quite India torn free to float in the Bay of Bengal— this is Pi.

A villager herded cows across the road, the milk white creatures casting an indifferent glance at the car. Renu stuck out her head to breathe deep the odor of cow, grass, dung, the sharp breath of Pi. Soon they were on the narrow lane that led to Nirmila Nivasam, rising from a sweep of lawn and garden. Whitewashed, with faded green shutters, a large veranda surrounding it on three sides, the house resembled a lopsided ship from a distance. Pots of chrysanthemums and roses lined the steps to the great carved door, always left open. On one side of the house, bougainvillaea grew in five wandering directions like a purple hand.

Bala, a flying figure in a voluminous sari, rushed down the steps to fix her sister and nieces with wet kisses, firing a dozen questions. Not waiting for answers, she began to check the girls' heads for fever. She stopped short at the sight of Renu's younger sister, dressed in a black T-shirt and black pants, her hair roughly razor-shorn.

"Meenakshi? You look like a boy," said Bala.

"My name is Manx," said Renu's sister.

"Look who's here from America," said their aunt, ushering them into Grandfather Das's room. He lay in bed studying his granddaughters for a long while before turning his head away. He seemed a stranger; nearly nine years had passed since Renu had last seen him, and in those years he'd changed so much. Gone was the stern taskmaster who had demanded she study hard, apply herself to books, and *learn*. Gone was the man who could make his mouth a grimace, a thin line that judged the entire world. Now he lay in bed, bald, shrunken, calm. He was preparing for his death; he had been in bed for the past three years, reciting Sanskrit, following all manner of prayers. Each night he slept as if it would be his last, and morning found him glaring at the new day. "For ninety years I have moved about—why should I continue?" he asked.

Adda entered the room to greet them next. He was the family rake, the uncle who had left Pi in the thirties to bring back a Spanish bride, who lived his life against the family's wishes. He looked at his father in bed and whispered to Renu, "Thirty years from now will find me walking, smoking, *living*."

In the next room, Rajesh's mother, Chitra, was inconsolable. Upon the death of her son, she'd unbound her hair, closed her door, and scratched at the walls with her fingernails in the fury of her grief. Rukmani entered the room to find her sister trying to stuff her mouth with the curtains. Bala hurried Renu away.

Renu unpacked after lunch. Manx collapsed on the bed as the ceiling fan sent cool breezes around. Fifteen, self-absorbed, and immensely bored, Manx had the ability to fall asleep anywhere, anytime. Renu put away her clothes and could not help keeping her ears alert, waiting for the familiar step. Breathlessly, he'd run in and tell them to rush, *vadis, vadis* in the half-Tamil, half-English he invented which his mother frowned upon, *c'mon you girls, let's polam, you're too slow, I've got tickets for the cinema*—but Renu stopped herself, it was crazy. How easy it would be to slip into the past, wade in nostalgia. She was not going to lose herself in this house of grief, where even the ever-present radio had been switched off. Renu opened Manx's suitcase where among blouses and trousers, her sister had packed jars and jars of peanut butter.

The cremation had been held the day before they'd arrived. Rajesh's body had been taken to the water's edge, lit with flame, and the ashes flung away. The crazy women mourners whose life it was to scream and wail for the dead lifted their arms as the wind carried her cousin's body away. The men watched the ashes dissolve: *Let your eyes go to the sun; your life to the wind; by the meritorious acts that you have done, go to heaven then to earth again* were the words of the cremation mantra. People on the riverbanks watched as they watched for each body that is scattered over the water, joining other bodies whose ashes might touch the river's bottom. But it wasn't the voices of a multitude that haunted Renu, only her cousin's voice, a single, recognizable sound, that drew her from her waking and sleep.

On the first night, Renu dreamed of Rajesh as she'd never seen him, a boy of nineteen, his hair lifting in the breeze. He walked with measured steps around and around the stone-smooth lip of the garden well. His foot fit exactly each brick's length, then raised in a curve of arch, the jutting of an ankle bone, before falling flat on the surface. She woke trembling and heard her aunt's fingernails on the walls. Renu got into Manx's bed where she slept in a tight curl.

Renu's mother wanted to take Chitra on a trip, to a hill station in south India or one in Sri Lanka. She said her sister needed to get away, to recover. Chitra sat against the wall as Rukmani talked, scrunched over, her head on her knees. A frail woman whose veins burned blue under her skin, Chitra viewed the roll of life as a series of punishments. She had lost her husband a year before Renu's father had died, and now, with the loss of her son, the jewel of her heart, she was desolate.

Chitra was the child who remained at home while Adda, Bala, and Rukmani tripped in and out as they grew. She was the one with the artistic temperament, the one prone to crying and headaches, the musical prodigy who didn't go to college but stayed at home to practice veena. At the time of her proposed tour with the National Ensemble, Chitra's father had put his foot down. No daughter of his was going to tramp across south India, travel on trains, eat at strange hotels. Her body had crumpled when told the news, and had never stopped shrinking. Even now her body was getting smaller, folding into itself in sorrow.

So much was different on Pi. Here no gesture was private, the sweep of family buffered all movement, all thoughts. Everything was discussed except family secrets. It had been another thing in New York. Renu's parents were scientists and their lives were austere, defined, tangible. One lived, one ate, one read newspapers, and rarely trusted anyone. "You were born in the space age," their father would say, and Renu and Manx grew up believing they could become astronauts. Except for a shelf of ivories and bronzes depicting dancing gods, there was no trace of Pi in their house on Long Island.

When their father died, Renu was fifteen, Manx, eleven. The family expected their mother to return to Pi, but she continued to work as a chemist at Stony Brook. The house changed, though, with their father's death. The Americanization and Westernization with which he'd tried so hard to shape their lives began to fall away. Aerogrammes from Pi reintroduced myth into their lives, stories he'd banished. From the aunts came good-day charts and advice. This is how to prevent indigestion, they wrote, this is how to cure cramps. Wean babies from milking breasts by rubbing wormwood on the nipples, they suggested, believing it was never too early to learn the lore of motherhood. They sent holy ash and *kungamum* blessed by the priests. Renu's mother began to pray regularly and attend the new Hindu temple in the city. The cabinets were filled with strange herbs and roots, medicinal cures and home remedies. Rukmani put away her coordinated pantsuits and wore saris from Lexington Avenue under her lab coats. She curtailed the girls' activities, refusing to allow them dances and late nights. The three of them drew together, gathering in the living room as one read, one knitted, one watched television. It was to be close to the other two that Renu declined an out-of-state scholarship and chose to go to a local college, attending classes as a day student.

Manx was offered a job in a record store in the mall, which her mother refused to let her take unless Renu worked there as well. So Renu worked part-time at a Chinese gift shop two doors down. If, on a break, Manx saw Renu dusting lacquered curios, she pretended not to know her. Rukmani came home to dinner weary and anxious and spoke of leaving her job.

For ten days following Rajesh's cremation, the holy light remained unlit in the shrine room. For ten days no one visited the house, the servants were sent away, and no one talked excessively. All movement was carefully planned, each step contained.

Renu met her aunt Chitra in the hallway once. "Renu-ma," sighed Chitra, leaning toward her.

She wishes it were me, thought Renu. She couldn't help it, there was something in her aunt's eyes, slightly accusing and indignant which Renu felt more than saw, sensed as her aunt held her. She could smell the shika root in her hair, the saltiness of her tears. Long after Chitra left her, Renu recalled the squashed eyes, the lines on her forehead, the grey hair she didn't hide with dye the way her own mother did, the loss in her face. If it had been me, thought Renu, it would be my mother he'd have to face, her eyes he'd have to pass by. But it was Rajesh who fell, whose body shuddered in spasms of pain, who had been wedged between steel and iron, or maybe he'd died quickly, instantly, hitting his head and losing all to darkness. The idea of death was so abstract to her that she wanted to seize all the possibilities of his dying, hold them like clues.

She dreamed Rajesh in water: his clothes bubbling like a pregnant woman's dress, his hair in misty disorder, his eyes turning to black pearls. His body clean, no cuts. If there had been any cuts, the red had streamed away. It was a preserved death, an odd death. There was no difference in the drowned person, the face untouched by blemish, bloating, or disfigurement, and it was only that the skin had turned hard, like glittering rock.

Renu awakened and lay in the darkness, trying to think of ways to entice sleep. When younger, she and Manx were bidden by their mother to dream of green fields and yellow flowers. Renu at ten closed her eyes and saw spiders and snakes. In their first American home, an apartment with a fire escape outside her bedroom window, she never saw the ladder for descent, only for something's way up. Renu would say a hurried prayer to ward against nightmares and plead with the gods: Please don't let me die before I see my cousin again. She'd wake with bags under her eyes.

Here on Pi, she told Bala that she had strange dreams at night. Bala said they were vision dreams. There were sages who had this gift of sight—the *Illustrated Weekly* claimed there were twelve-year-old boys who had holy ash fall out of their ears at night, who woke up with prophecy. Renu never paid attention to these stories, attributing their power to the throng of faithful who wished to believe, who needed something to be awed by. Still, there were her dreams. Bala said it had to do with her diet. Manx was certain Renu was a fortune-teller and wanted her palms read.

"Don't be stupid," said Renu.

"I want to know my chosen path, I want order," said Manx. "It saves time."

Renu began to wash her clothes daily, rubbing her shirts across a broad stone under an outside tap, rubbing the collars until her hands were raw and red. She was determined to stay clean, never mind that her shirts seemed to turn filthy after a day's wearing. Nothing she did could get rid of that smell of death. Sometimes she rubbed so hard she almost ripped the cloth, and sometimes she wished she could. Tear it apart, wrench it open so there would be a hole at the heart so it could fall useless to her feet. She rinsed the clothes with cold water and hung them up; they blew in the wind like full sails.

"When I was little, Rajesh promised me we could all live in a palace made of ice cream. If we got hungry, we could nibble on a window ledge or a doorknob. Everyone would have their own room and balcony, but I was only five or so, and scared of balconies. Rajesh said we could share a room, but he would still get his own balcony, where he was going to set up a big telescope to see all the way to Neptune."

Renu had heard the story before, but she didn't stop Manx from telling it. She liked the repetition, the rhythm of the words. If she listened hard enough, she could catch different tremors in her voice, sift memory from truth. She was jealous of memories of Rajesh. She wanted to hear each story about him over and over, so that she could re-create his entire life. If Aunt Bala spoke of him cramming ("mugging") for exams, she wanted to see him leaning over his books, coffee steaming from a cup nearby. She wanted to see him walking into town, drinking a bottle of Kami Cola, sneaking a cigarette, then chewing peppermint gum so his mother wouldn't know. But there was always something elusive, gaps she couldn't fill, moments denied her, his twin-cousin.

Sometimes they'd had pantomimes, acting out pieces of comic book adventures or myths. Guess who this is, she'd say, turning up one palm, the other strumming an imaginary sitar, then switching to imitate the third and fourth hands of the wisdom goddess. Rajesh would pretend to be Garuda, the heavenly hero bird, shaking massive green wings, assuming a terrible pose. If Manx was around, she'd be assigned a minimal role, a sleeping baby Krishna, a holy tree. "You guys were so boring," Manx would say later.

The rain had followed them from New York. Here, water dripped from leaf to leaf in distinct *tap-taps*. Everything became brighter, clearer, as the earth soaked in the rain. Villagers hurried under makeshift umbrellas of overturned baskets and children sheltered themselves beneath large banana leaves. Cows ambled by with their white knees streaked with red mud. There was no fog to hide anything. The plants had a waxy look, the wet flowers seemed less real, as if they were newly created and ready to fall at once.

Renu didn't dare to think of rebirth. That was Aunt Bala's trap; she could look at an ant or spider and see the resemblance to Akbar or Napoleon. *Go to heaven and the earth again; remain in the herbs with the bodies you propose to take.* Could Rajesh come back as a plant? Could he nod his petaled head alongside a path? Would he be a particular flower, near a rock striped a certain way, on a specific dust-covered path, or would his soul be sifted over an entire bed of blooms? She asked her grandfather.

"The scholars argue about this. Generally, one soul or single self transposes into another single self, but can the body of an ant, so small, a dot, contain the spirit of what was once a man? Yes, because you see there is no such thing as dimension. You know we are all nearly imperceptible to the gods, and they themselves are trivial in comparison with the Divine Breath," he said.

"All of which is bullshit," said Uncle Adda later. "Let me tell you a story. They say that Vishnu contains the entire universe within him in slumber, and that our existence is his dream. One day, a sage who was walking about in the world chanced to slip out of Vishnu's mouth, which hung slightly open in sleep. The sage found himself in a strange ocean, a world existing outside of his own existence, a non-universe. To be within Vishnu, he was part of a dream, but to be outside was not to exist at all. Which, then, is reality?"

Adda wetted the end of the pencil he held. "See? We paint ourselves into a corner all the time. We make ourselves powerless with queries such as these. Which is reality? Why should anyone bother with that?"

Renu watched as her uncle wandered into the garden. It was said that if Adda was presented with the riddle of the Sphinx, he would not only answer the monster's question but ask a dozen in return. Bala scoffed at the idea, though. If the Sphinx were to pose her a question, she'd waste no time in running away. "What fool would hang around with trouble so near?" she said.

Adda stood in front of a banyan tree. With his pencil, he was scratching dreamily on the soft bark. Bala came outside and saw him.

"What are you doing?" she yelled. "Why are you killing my tree?"

"I just had a thought," he said.

"As if that's enough reason to draw on a tree?"

"Nature," he told Renu as he strode disgustedly into the house, "has always stood in the path of science."

At night, Renu heard moaning, soft guttural gasps that sometimes sounded like rain, but suddenly pulled away and stood by itself so there was no denying what it was. She never knew if the sound of pain came from outside, from her dreams, or from her aunt's sorrow. The grief of the house made it possible to steer movement into ritual, to act without explanation. Chitra and Rukmani took their meals separately. Grandfather

Das chanted for hours, Manx sat on the veranda with her Walkman plugged in. Renu couldn't shake the sleep from her eyes until noon, even though she waked much earlier. Sometimes she felt as if she were still in a dream, seeing the world through a veil. Her relatives seemed remote figures who had no bearing on her life. Once, she watched the cook cutting vegetables, sitting on the floor, passing eggplant through a fixed carving blade; so clean, so pure was the movement that Renu felt she could pass her hand through the blade and nothing would happen, there would be no harm. She leaned forward to try but Manx came up suddenly behind her and jostled her to safety.

On the thirteenth day, they feasted. The curtains were pulled back, the servants returned, the house was scrubbed clean. Buckets of water were poured on the porch to chase the dust away. Pots of food were cooked, sweets were fried, and bunches of flowers were collected for the shrine room. Relatives and friends descended from all over to celebrate the soul's passage from life to life. Children ran shouting through the halls.

People crowded into every room, pushing out the sorrow. They asked the girls question after question: How old are you now? Are you taller than your sister—let's see, stand straight. Do you miss New York? Does it snow a lot? When did you begin to menstruate? You look so skinny, is that the American fashion? Midway, Manx escaped to town with Uncle Adda, and returned with her arms full of every American magazine she could find.

Someone sang a song to ease a two-year-old to sleep. In one room, all the women were talking, eating handfuls of *murruku* and peanuts, arguing about the laziness of a new maid, how much to pay the sweetmaker. Renu's mother, thinner and older in a matter of days, sat with her knees alongside the knees of Chitra, who sat still and silent. In another room, all the men were sleeping as babies played at their feet. One of the cousins put on a disco record, and she and Manx danced in the kitchen.

The house was breathing again, lifting itself out of mourning. Noise found its way into every corner, every closet, every forgotten hiding place. Renu had to go deep into the garden, past the mimosa tree, past the lemon trees, where only the monkeys could hear her as she let out scream after scream.

Three

They found her in the garden and put her to bed. For three days she was confined, her body bursting with chills and fevers. Bala and Manx kept constant vigil, while others of the household drifted in and out.

When the doctor came, a man who had been treating the family since the aunts were girls, he pronounced it nothing more than heat stroke and exhaustion. He advised complete rest and several hours a day in the garden. "Once she smells the soil and breathes the fresh air, her body will acclimatize and restore itself," he said.

Nevertheless, Chitra stood by Renu's bed and wrung her hands. "My god, my dearest sister, imagine losing our babies so young," she wailed to Renu's mother. Nothing could dissuade her; she was convinced that Renu's death was a matter of course. She sighed heavily and patted her sister's hand. "We must be very brave," she said.

So nearly three weeks after her arrival, Renu found herself in a comfortable wicker chair to recuperate in the garden. From her seat, she could watch the comings and goings of the household, watch the minute growth of the garden greenery, follow the early sun's travel through the sky until it became too hot for her to sit further.

She felt an encompassing vagueness around her, and nothing seemed as it should be. She waited for the approaching heat of the day, aware of her skin's sensitive prickling whenever a stray breeze happened to wander, heard all the noise around her. Still, Renu felt as if she was far away, wearing glasses that weren't quite clear. She shook her head, wanting to wake up. She tried to recall dates from Art History, the dimensions of famous buildings, as if they could help place her in the world. She thought she was spinning around, an errant satellite in need of a motherly body, something large to use as a fixed point, something to guide her path.

At times, various family members came to sit with her. Bala brought out baskets of peas to shell, told stories, bits of family history, but Renu had no desire for conversation.

When the sun grew too hot, she went inside where everyone stretched out on sleeping mats under the fans to escape the heat. The rushes that were woven into curtains were drawn around the porch and soaked with water, perfuming the air with each passing breeze. The languidness of the days washed over Renu like a warm bath. She thought of the endless hours spent by island women drinking tea, lazily gossiping, watching the sun sink day after day.

She became an attentive observer in the garden. She was aware of the subtlest change of light, a heightened moment when each dust mote was outlined brilliantly in the air, and everything became bright and clear, as if something momentous was going to take place, as if she were on the threshold of infinite understanding, but then the moment would pass, and she would be left with nothing more than the afternoon.

No matter how discreet they tried to be, there was no denying it; everyone watched Renu carefully. Bala inspected each dish the cook prepared, peering at the fully steamed rice, sifting suspiciously through the sauces and vegetables, making sure no stone had wandered in by mistake, no dirt slipped in undetected. Her niece would not die of food poisoning if she could help it.

Renu made no protest as her aunt checked her plate for impurities. Manx silently spread peanut butter on shop-bought white bread. Renu hardly tasted her food, letting it pass through her mouth as her mind turned ever more inward, lost in a net of nostalgia.

If Bala was overcautious, Rukmani seemed resigned to the fate that was going to take her eldest from her. It wasn't merely her sister's persuasion; Rukmani knew that the gods were greedy, and if they were due two, they would not rest easy with one.

"Would you like to do anything special, Renu-ma? Go to Kashmir and ride horses the way we did when you were a little girl? Why don't you travel with Auntie and me? We could have a lot of fun," she'd say to her daughter, passing a hand distractedly through Renu's hair.

But on no account did Renu want to travel with her mother and aunt. She could imagine such a trip, with her mother trying to make each moment *matter* and her aunt wringing her hands desperately. All Renu wanted was to be left alone with remembrance.

Dear Renu. You can't possibly imagine how hot it is here. I wish it would snow, I'd like to shovel the driveway. Thanks for the books, I like the Tolkien especially. Have you ever read "The Overcoat"? It's a fantastic story. Well, Aunt Bala is cursing out a goat now. The damn thing insists on eating her roses. I told her it doesn't know not to do it, but she shakes her broom at me! I like my class a little better this year. Pundi doesn't bother me anymore, he's such an ass anyway . . .

Dear Renu. Guess what? I'm going to Colombo for the hols, along with Muru and Ravi. Five days and no work! What were the Catskills like? Did you go hiking and climbing? There are girl guides here, too, but most go to St. Mary's and are absolute prisses. How is Meena these days? Tell her that her cousin-brother says hello. Oh, I got a nice present from Uncle—a damn good set of straight edges, a lovely compass, a mechanical pencil—I think they belonged to his wife . . .

As always, night terrified her. In bed, calmed with water that had been first boiled, then cooled in earthen cisterns, Renu would wait for sleep. Her eyes would seem to know peace for only a few minutes before she was caught in a sudden dream. Three women would materialize at the foot of her bed, giantesses whom she never saw completely, only their faces, or hands, or laps. They looked like no one she knew, yet they would gather near her to place stones in their mouths and swallow. She could see the stones funnel down their bodies, the way one could trace an egg's progress to the belly of a snake. Sometimes only one woman appeared, a woman with a big stomach, with long pale hair and empty hands. She just stared at Renu. Renu tossed in the confusion of her dreams, rocked in meanings that escaped her.

Nighttime, and the outside winds whistled. A flock of birds, upset by the change in weather, set up a terrible clamor. There must have been a hundred birds, disturbed from their roost, all aflight at once. Then the cats began, moaning eerily as witches. The noise strummed through her arms, which ached with pressure. The fact that the house was filled with sleeping bodies was of no help to Renu; slumber eluded her.

She tried tricks. She imagined her body dissolving into the sheets like liquid Jell-O. She concentrated on a single image to be lulled into sleep. She imagined the celestial cobra spreading its hood over her in protection as it did for the resting

Vishnu, but it was of no use. Soon those jaws opened, soon those fangs flashed. So frightened was she when she scared herself awake, so bathed was her back in sweat, that she began to keep the lights on. She pushed her bed up close to Manx's, hugged a pillow to her chest.

Sleep would not come to her either in the glare of the day. So she sat in the garden, drifting into reverie, spending hours imagining Rajesh's footfall, what she might say to him if he appeared, what he would say. With half her mind she knew she was crazy to indulge, but the sweetness of the memory, the way she could float so easily into the past and pass time there was so pleasurable, she couldn't bear to stop. Like an addict with a secret cache of chemicals, she whet her desire frequently.

Four

Manx lost her watch. It wasn't precious, just something she'd picked up in a quick-stop store on Long Island. The store peddled bright cakes and candies, warm and cold beer, acrylic visor caps, sunglasses that folded up, plastic combs guaranteed for a lifetime, tiny tins full of aspirin, transparent water guns, personal horoscopes, miniature sewing kits for travel, cards full of needles, cures for colds and allergies, and a dozen varieties of chewing gum. On the counter, between a jar filled with buttons featuring the faces of pop stars and a canister of rubber worms, was a display of two-dollar watches that ran for a year, no questions asked. She had selected a chartreuse model with a black, numberless face.

Manx asked the cook if she'd seen the watch.

"Ask Brindani," was the preoccupied reply.

In stumbling Tamil, Manx asked the servant girl about the watch. Brindani had just returned to work that morning after a three-day absence ministering to her brother, who'd been beaten up by the police. Lacking sleep, terrified for her brother's situation, and tired of questions, Brindani blinked at Manx and burst into tears. Manx was bewildered and stood there speechless. Bala, attracted by the commotion, tried to appease the girl while Manx muttered, "It's just a dumb watch."

As Manx sulked out of the room, Bala thought of the difference between her nieces. If Renu had been involved, she would have spent several days in mortification and apology, enlarging the incident out of proportion, while Manx on the other hand would seek no explanation, and shrug it all off as yet another example of the unfathomable island culture.

"Well, after all, she's just a child," said Bala to Brindani.

"They're so weird," Manx told Renu.

"What did you do?"

Manx's mouth hung open for a second. In New York, her teeth would have been flecked with bits of bright pink lipgloss as she chewed her lips angrily. Here, they seemed vulnerable in their bareness.

"Nothing."

"What do you need a watch for anyway?" asked her grandfather.

"I like to know the time."

"There's only one time worth knowing, and that's the day this land sinks," said her grandfather.

"That's a long way off," said Manx.

"What's the point of keeping track in the meanwhile?"

"Grandpa, I want to know how much time I've got."

"You Americans want to own everything. My old friend Ramamurthy used to keep an appointment book when he was vice president of a major corporation in Chicago, a city no less worthy than New York, they say. He had a book that showed three lines for every quarter-hour of the day, so he could claim and account for each portion of the day before he dismissed it for the next. He even wrote when to take a pill."

"Some watches beep so you never forget to take a pill."

"At that time, he swallowed ten pills a day."

"Some watches have calculators, and some have mini-televisions, and some play music, and some have holograms and some speak to you." She made up the last two kinds.

"All you need to know is that it's nineteen hundred and eighty, according to the Christian calendar, and even that is questionable."

"Some are really telephones."

"Imagine taking ten pills a day."

Manx wandered around. She felt bored and useless here. She wondered what her friends back home were doing. They were probably at the Metro, flipping through the record bins. Nothing was fair. It was a stupid world.

She found Renu in Rajesh's old room. No one went in it anymore except her sister. Renu was sitting in a chair, looking blankly into space. Her sister was crazy.

Manx was about to turn around and leave, when she caught sight of something on the floor. It was a baby bird. The color of chalky peach, a quivering mass of skin, it lay with one eye bulging, as if ready to spill out. Manx shuddered. It was entirely helpless.

"Do you see it?" asked Manx.

But Renu made no reply, so Manx faced the bird alone. It had apparently fallen from the ceiling fan, where she could see bits of a nest between the blades. What a dumb mother, she thought. She knew that if she were to touch the birdlet, the mother might reject it, so she looked around for something to pick it up with. Taking two sticks, Manx maneuvered the bird onto a plate, and carried it out to the garden. Now what? If she left it out in the open, it would be vulnerable to predators. She decided to place it on the tulsi plant stand; the stone pot in which the herb grew was set on a pedestal, so it was high as well as holy.

When she told her grandfather, he shrugged. "Seems simpler just to wring its neck."

"Imagine him going at his age!" shouted Aunt Bala.

Manx woke to a household in disarray. She was sleepy; Renu had had a bad night. Now, everyone was shouting.

Bala was pacing nervously in the kitchen.

"A lot of people go to Trivandur," said Adda, cleaning bottles. He was building a model of the city palace at Jaipur out of tiny medicine bottles.

"He's been in bed so long, his knees will give in—what if his knees give in?" said Bala.

"He'll take a bus most of the way and a bus will bring him back," said Adda.

"Do you think he even thought to pack a lunch? He should have told me," said Bala. "And for God's sake, can't you stop making toys for once and do something?"

Adda was about to reply when Manx walked into the kitchen. "Maybe he told Meena-ma."

"Told me what?" asked Manx.

"Your grandfather has gone to Trivandur!" shouted her aunt, throwing up her hands. "He's gone to Trivandur to break his knees!"

Manx was startled. Although he had insisted that he was going to make a pilgrimage one day, she never thought it more than a vague threat. Trivandur's temple, located on a hill in the northern outskirts of the city, accessible by five hundred steep steps cut out of stone, attracted hundreds of visitors, including the fiercest devotees. There was a woman who made the climb twice daily, carrying a brass vessel filled with oranges on her head, another vessel at one hip, and her baby on the other. She walked up the steps without pause, passing others who rested every dozen steps or so. One man made the climb on his hands while two snakes entwined themselves at his feet. Legend insisted that a man clothed only in prayer beads had once made the journey accompanied by a tiger.

Less spectacular worshipers flocked to the temple as well, carrying trays of coconuts, delicate sweets, garlands of flowers to offer the god of the temple. Year-old babies were brought to have their heads shaved for luck and the dying came to seek final blessings on earth. The god at Trivandur was so powerful that the eyes of his image were half-covered, such was their intensity. Manx had been scared of this god when younger, preferring butter-eyed Ganesha and open-mouthed Krishna. Now a professed atheist, she was still confounded by her grandfather's preference for the sterner god. Perhaps he was good to the old.

Manx looked through an album of photographs. Renu must have gone through it already, for there were many blanks where pictures ought to have been. There was one of her grandfather with her grandmother and all their children. Everyone looked distracted, except for her grandfather, who faced the camera. Adda had a funny half-grin on his face, as if he were inventing excuses to stay away from school the next day. Bala had blinked as the light had flashed, Rukmani was playing with her braids, and Chitra smiled at the ground. Manx returned to her grandfather; he stood so straight, his face smooth, a few wisps of hair over his forehead. Years ago, he had told her the story of how a god had one day leaned out of a celestial window and seen a squirrel. Pleased with the tiny creature, he reached down to pet it. His godly fingers left three strokes on the animal's back, imprints of his power. Thus, the chipmunk. Some god must have sneaked into her grandfather's room, Manx thought, to stroke his face, to cut wrinkles deep as scars.

The day was hot, even for the season of fire. For two months each year, the sun beat relentlessly on the island, burning leaves and vines at a touch, draining gullies and streams. In the garden, the asoka trees were quiet, no breeze rippled their whispery leaves. Manx tested the heat by placing one bare foot on the ground. She stifled a scream, afraid to touch her reddened sole. She waited for blisters to appear. When none did, she gazed instead at the day's thick heat. There were one hundred ways to die in the sun, and thirty-three kinds of heat stroke.

Bala asked Manx to help cut vegetables for the evening meal. As her aunt turned the huge mortar to grind the rice to flour, Manx split beans. They cracked under her fingers like insect wings.

"I wonder if he took a water jug," mused her aunt.

"Maybe he'll pick up some food on the road," said Manx.

"Oh, ya, *bajjis* cooked in kerosene," grumbled her aunt.

Manx closed her eyes and saw a praying mantis die. She opened them to make the image disappear.

"He'll probably come home with jaundice," said her aunt.

Who didn't come to Nirmila Nivasam once the great door opened at dawn? The vendors, the dancers, the village soothsayers, snakers, portrait artists, holy beggars to plead for their temples. And the banana seller, an old woman who arrived once a week, carrying small, sweet fruit bruised by the basket. She sat on the steps, massaging her feet stained with dust from the road as Manx looked over her wares.

"So your grandfather has gone to Trivandur?"

Manx wondered how she knew.

"He shouldn't have gone by himself."

"He can take care of himself—it's not that far," said Manx.

The woman placed her hand on Manx's knee. "So you say," she said. "These old men, they look past their faces one day in the mirror and decide they need to see God. I know these men. They get scared. Your grandfather has been in bed for three years waiting for God to nod yes, and then he gets scared."

Manx's knee was growing uncomfortably damp.

"My husband went to Trivandur—he went to the river to bathe first, as he had done every morning of his life, and then went to Trivandur, and dropped dead on the road. Just like that, nothing else, he dropped dead and died. *Aiyo, Rama*, he died—"

The woman was rocking now, wringing her sadness out like water. Manx began to rock, too.

"*Aiyo, Rama*, he died, he died—"

Manx nodded and rocked.

"And you tell me, what was I supposed to do after that?"

Perhaps he was now climbing the hill, Manx thought, maybe breathing heavily, even panting. Other devotees, mostly younger, would pass him. Up, up, foot after foot on stone, past the hawker stands selling cheap curios and beads, little models of the temple that lit up, past the minor shrines, until finally, the darkness of a rock-cut temple, the bronze and gold ornaments gone black with smoke a thousand years old, and all the splendor of the image within. Maybe a wide-eyed foreigner would mistake his white dhoti, his worn sandals, his gleaming baldness for the costume of a holy man and bow for blessings. Would he smile like a priest, benign, all-knowing, just short of smug?

Or maybe he would undergo transformation after his visit, like Gregor Samsa. Maybe her grandfather would become taller, or grow broad shoulders. Maybe he was placing coins in the hands of the beggars he usually ignored. The dusty bus ride, the sultry climb up and down the hill, indefinite conversations with strangers—the journey should have lasted only a few hours. Did he think he had time to stop for every open palm in Trivandur?

. . .

"Renu, do you want to play backgammon?"

"No."

"My god, Bala, you can't call the police because a man has gone to temple. You should be the last one to begrudge a man his religion." Adda was on the porch, adding a gold-blue minaret to his tabletop palace.

"He could get a stroke—he might have already had one," whispered his sister.

Manx gazed at herself in the bathroom mirror. Her hair, buzzed with a razor a month back, was definitely getting unruly. She made a paste of tooth powder in her palm and brushed her teeth. Unlike baking soda, which her mother always pushed, the powder had a pleasant taste. Manx brushed again for the taste. Then she took a pair of scissors and snipped. Locks of hair fell into the sink.

"Go ahead. Go ahead and cut off more."

Her aunt Bala was staring at her, her face ashen. "Go ahead and shave it all off!"

Manx had never seen her aunt so furious. She wondered if Bala would hit her. She looked as if she might. Manx kept still. But as abruptly as she'd entered, her aunt left. Manx continued to cut her hair.

Manx dragged a ladder into Rajesh's old room. She placed it under the fan and began to climb up. The baby bird had disappeared from the tulsi plant. She wondered if someone had killed it, or if a cat had eaten it. She wondered if there were others.

She peered at the dusty blades of the fan. The nest, near the motor, was a ragtail construction of twigs and thready straw. It was empty, but when Manx lifted it out, she saw woven into its side a bit of plastic. Her watch. She buried the whole lot under the tulsi plant.

Manx dreamed of climbing hills, groping on her knees; like a devotee she climbed up the grassy incline. Someone was calling her "Meenakshi." The sun was stinging her eyes, making rivers of sweat run down her forehead, her arms. Now the sun was sending fiery arrows to pierce her—she woke from the pain. Manx sat up in the dark room. Mosquito bites made bumps along her arms. Everything was still and hot. The electricity had gone off.

She went outside, where most of the family had gathered. Long incense sticks were lit to keep the mosquitoes away, and someone was spraying bug repellant. The neighborhood was awake, the season too hot for sleep during a government current-rationing blackout. A murmur of voices drifted near the gate as neighbors patrolled the area to make sure everyone was suffering equally. A card table was set up and a deck was cut.

Manx imagined that this tableau would last forever. That her aunts would always chatter and gossip, her sister remain catatonic, her grandfather absent. If she were to hold her breath, if she never uttered another sound, it would still be the same. The moon flicked in and out of the clouds, soundlessly fishing the sky.

There was a sudden rattle at the gate, a shuffle of feet. Her grandfather stood before them, returned from his trek. He had dried sandalwood paste on his arms, red and ash powder on his forehead. His feet were dirty and swollen.

"The island is sinking," he announced. "The god told me there is nothing to be done."

Five

Upholding the circle that used to be her family was what Renu did. She stretched out her arms, palms cupped, and demanded they float within that span, that they be content to remain in a freeze-frame of her needs. All those evenings spent on Long Island after her father's death, three women in the living room, the lethargy it inspired, seemed part of an immobile tapestry. It was an especially Krishnan reaction, Renu felt, to turn ever inward to the family, exclusive of all outside elements.

American life was different, she was convinced, feeling that difference deeply. Renu believed that American parents stood by their child's room at night, gazing with delight at the sleeping form, at the nicely matched furniture, the walls covered with pennants and posters, and the obligatory collection of athletic awards, smiling: this was their child. But knowing, too, that once the child was colleged, they could repanel the walls, cover the crayon marks, and convert the room into a needed den or exercise room. This was the American way, to raise children and let them go, an independence nurtured by the first after-school job, the first date, the carousing nights with friends (and here she always imagined teenage boys and girls eating hot dogs in a bright kitchen while parents slept trustingly upstairs). The hugs at high school graduation were traditional, taken-for-granted part-ings, Renu believed, partings that would never be given so willingly by island parents.

Island girls were expected to follow the rules, behave them-selves within and outside the family, save themselves for the sanctity of marriage. No boys, no questions. The early re-bellions were reined in by their father's death, and Renu reacted by throwing herself to the task of preserving the family. She watched her mother closely for signs of crack-up, taking over the cooking to assure that meals would be served regularly. Losing contact with friends, letting the phone alone, it was easy to reduce the circumference of her world. But nothing could stop the slow flush creeping up her throat in high school, inventing excuses, I have to baby-sit, I have chores, I must study, saying no to excursions and dances. Island girls do not date, her mother had said, crisply, severely, no more nonsense. What did they do? They theorize, they rationalize, they become computer science majors if they can-not be doctors. In college, it was easy to shrug off friendships, adjust to the routine of sleeping, eating, doing coursework, working, watching television. It was the same on Pi really, a schedule of activities lazily followed, and all the necessities taken care of.

In the garden, Renu reflected on the changes precipitated by their move to America. She thought about her parents' capacity for adaptation, how her mother weathered the tran-sition. As a young girl who had family and servants to cater to all her needs, a woman who had never been to market by herself, her mother had held her breath and willy-nilly left the island for America, land of the self-serve.

There she bravely walked down the aisles of supermarkets, taking in the seemingly endless supply of frozen foods, juice concentrates, canned cheeses, and boxes of cereal with free toys inside. She pushed the smart steel carts, marveling at their oiled smoothness, filling them with celebrated TV dinners. She tried to figure out the appliances in the kitchen, the toaster that didn't really work, the temperamental mixer, discovering she'd bought all the wrong things, trying to make a simple *dāl* with incorrect beans and dinner having to wait hours, everyone upset and bothered and hungry.

What an enormous amount she learned. Instead of handing her clothes to a waiting dhobi, she encountered monstrous machines that she must feed and empty; she had to sort and arrange clothes according to washability; select a special detergent and appropriate water temperature after consulting some charts, a bleach, a fabric softener. She could add a no-static cling paper to the load, or let it rest and hope for the best. Her mother moved through American life, tough as a pioneer, conquering dryers, parking meters, elevators, cellophane-packed goods, soda dispensers, checkout lines, gas stations, and car washes. Renu wasn't sure she could have coped, had she been in her mother's shoes.

So sat Renu thinking when her mother came outside, eyes and sari gleaming.

"Renu-ma, there you are, I've found you," said her mother.

"I was just sitting."

Renu's mother dropped into a chair nearby but couldn't resist jumping up and giving her daughter—clever perfect darling firstborn—a quick kiss.

"Oh, my darling, I'm so happy to see you. Listen, you are so young, so full of promise—you have such a good life ahead of you, such joy. I was misled by Chitra, the poor dear, but now I see. Yes, and the only happiness I have in this world is to see you happy."

Renu wondered what her mother was leading up to.

"Oh, my angel, I have decided, I have absolutely decided, it's time to get you settled." Rukmani leaned back and waited for her daughter's response.

"Marriage? Mom?"

But her mother simply beamed at her.

"I'm not even twenty yet."

"But you will be soon. You can finish your studies here, and just get *engaged* now. Then with your degree in hand, you can settle down somewhere. We'll find you a nice doctor, or a promising engineer, and why, you can even work if you want to. We are a very modern family, after all."

Getting up, the matter presumably settled, her mother kissed Renu again and left, her feet hardly touching the ground.

Rukmani thought marriage was not only proper and necessary for her daughter, but by speeding things along, it would offer a means of salvation and grace. She saw it as a party, a distracting, exciting spectacle that would take months of planning, shopping, issuing invitations, visiting, not to mention all the details to attend to in selecting a groom. With so much to do, Rukmani was certain that her daughter would be forced out of her melancholia.

Renu leaned back in her chair. What an idea. Marriage was a strange thing in her family, and disappointments were not uncommon. For one thing, most of the women tended to marry with their eyes shut. Statistics would reassure them, for as everyone knew, family-arranged marriages almost never ended in divorce. The bride's and groom's heights would nicely match, their tastes in food would be similar, their astrological signs would be in harmony—these details would be seized by the matchmakers and made much of by the parents. The bride-to-be was left to daydream, linger over a few minutes of meeting, and elaborate on her expectations. By the time of the wedding, a vision of a warrior, a shining cinema star, would dominate her thoughts as she bathed in sandalwood and rose petals. No wonder the women in her family photographs looked so grim, thought Renu—imagining Heathcliff and discovering only Kumar or Anand.

Her cousin Anu had broken the rules, marrying a German painter she'd met in Berlin. While the rest of her anthropology class wound its way to Florence, Anu ducked out from the doyenne-grip of Our Lady of Sacred Heart's sisters and remained in Germany. It had been a great scandal, but within a week, Anu had married Günter or Bruno, and had made the leap that untied her from her past.

She'd written to the Krishnans once, perhaps thinking that American relatives might be more sympathetic to her situation, but Renu's parents never discussed the letter. Renu knew of its existence only by the torn envelope with foreign stamps she'd found in a wastebasket. Copying the address, she herself had written to Anu, congratulating her and wondering if she, too, might come to Berlin. She asked Anu her opinion of the Beatles, and of Germany's attitude toward its Nazi past. She also listed twenty-three grievances against her parents and sister. She never mailed the letter.

For Anu, marrying out of caste and without approval meant exile, a complete discontinuation of the life she'd known on the island. No one attempted to contact her, and she became both a bright and extinguished light for Renu.

Her uncle Adda, however, had brought his bride back to the island, and no one could do anything about it. Aunt Bala sniffed when she told stories of the foreigner in the house, how pale and thin she was, a snob from the beginning. She died without giving Adda a child, and *that*, said Bala, was what happened when you marry out of caste. Adda himself would not speak of his wife, and Renu found herself wondering more and more about her Spanish aunt. What caused her to leave her homeland for the island, and what had she found upon arrival? Renu felt a funny closeness to this aunt; they shared the common bond of immigrants.

But there were others who had married well, who entered unions in which promises were fulfilled and wants met. It was an ancient system, based on the stars and the practical needs of each couple, and in most cases, infallible.

If Rajesh had lived, who would he have married? Someone she could get along with, that was certain. But to give up her place to some stranger girl, a housewifey type, was unthinkable. As for herself, well, it seemed implausible. Renu could not imagine marrying anyone. Maybe she was going to die soon, as everyone suspected, so perhaps marriage wasn't in her cards. Her mother seemed happy at the prospect, though, very intent on a wedding. It would be hard to disappoint her, but if she was going to die anyway, there was no reason why she shouldn't go along with the plan.

That night, Renu dreamed of a line of unmarried women partnered with apes, wandering down vast, empty lanes. When she woke up, she wondered where the image had come from, from the island or America, Art History or mythology? Did no one approve of unattached females?

When, a few days later, Rukmani approached her with a dish of her favorite sweets and a list of suitable boys, Renu could not say no. She gave her mother the okay to dispatch letters and consult horoscopes. Bala agreed with Rukmani: it was a fine idea. Only Adda shrugged and refused to comment.

Six

Manx sat by the vegetable market, shaking her radio furiously. For an hour she'd been trying to fine-tune the thing into function, but only static issued from its plastic power speaker. It seemed reasonable that a higher altitude would produce better reception, and the Madhupur market was set on a hillside, but the hit parade from the BBC could barely be made out. Although she disdained hit parades, even hearing the gummy sounds of England's latest teen idols was better than nothing. By being on the island, Manx felt that she was missing everything, that across the ocean, new and dizzying power was being wielded by songs she had no knowledge of. How would she catch up?

She ignored the stares and rude calls of the boys around her. One eager fellow tried to catch Manx's hand, saying, "You want to go to a film, baby?" but she pushed him away. I'm an ugly space monster, she said to herself, imagining spiky armor on her back, long green claws to ward off on-lookers. At first, she'd been surprised by the amount of leering on the streets, assuming island men had been taught the same restraint as island women. Keep your eyes down, and walk fast, she'd been told. Sexual division existed everywhere on the island, men and women almost aliens to each other. There were separate lines in the temples, at the movies, sometimes even for the buses. Under lurid movie posters featuring a hero grinning at a heroine's strangely pointed breasts, films that suggested sex by having the couple go behind a bush and having the bush shake wildly, groups of loitering men eyed women. The papers labeled sexual harassment as nothing more than "Eve teasing." "But you know," her mother had insisted when Manx brought up the subject, "an island man would never hurt an island girl—it doesn't happen here."

"Maybe I can help," said a voice above her.

"Fuck off," she was about to mutter when she realized the voice was American. Curious, she looked up to see a white man with his hair pulled back in a ponytail, wearing tiny round glasses.

But he wasn't addressing her. Manx watched as he collected packages that a woman in a pink and silver sari had dropped. The woman stood imperially, used to attendance, as he stooped to retrieve all of them. She received the packages without a word, and turning smartly on her heels, she entered a waiting car.

"That was Mirazi, Light of the World."

Now it appeared that he was speaking to Manx.

"What's a Mirazi?"

The man sighed before replying. He looked so forlorn, she wanted to giggle. Then he looked straight at Manx, steadily absorbing her face, her clothing, her youth, all at once. Strangely, her skin prickled and she very nearly blushed.

"Mirazi is the single most beautiful woman in the city. The Light of the World, the Rare Elixir of Womankind."

"You're kidding."

"No."

Manx wondered if she were a movie star.

"She seems like a snob, though," she said.

"That's her way," said the American. "I run into her every couple of weeks, but she's never alone. She always has this entourage around her, and gets driven in that '63 Falcon everywhere. This is the first time I've actually talked with her."

"How long have you been following her around?"

"Two years."

"Two *years?*"

The man nodded.

"What does she do?" asked Manx.

"Shops. Wanders around. She's a tea estate heiress, born of Indian parents in Brooklyn, educated in Switzerland. No one knows where she lives, she disappears for months."

He introduced himself as Freddie Flat, itinerant American. He had dropped out of college when his parents refused to pay tuition for classes he never attended; he supported himself with odd jobs until he had enough money for an Air India ticket. He hung out with the Beatles crowd a while, but when both the Maharishi and the group left, he'd emigrated to the island.

"I used to think I was looking for something, something to give everything shape, you know? But I've since figured that it's a matter of not seeking it directly, that the meaning will approach me as I live," he said as he fiddled with the dial on her radio.

"Yeah," said Manx, "I guess."

"Anyway, I've been away from the States for about fifteen years now, as long as you've been alive, probably." He handed her back the radio, which was surprisingly playing a song she liked.

"You like this stuff?" he asked.

"Yeah, it's great—thanks."

"It sounds so angry to me."

"That's why it's so great. I mean, if you're feeling awful and angry and mad, you need to listen to loud, loud music because it matches the way you feel. I mean, if you feel *good*, you can listen to anything, but when you don't, you feel better listening to this."

She wondered if he were a Deadhead. Or worse, a TMer.

"I'm Manx. I've got to go."

The next time Manx went to the market, she kept on glancing around her, but it wasn't until she saw him that she realized she'd been looking for Freddie. She joined him for a fake Coke at a milk bar. The café was a haunt of Mirazi's, he told her.

"So you're, like, her fan?"

He shrugged. It first started off as a fancy, a passing interest in this woman he kept seeing around town. But his obsession with the Light of the World was intensified by her oblivious-ness. Sometimes he'd wake in the morning just wondering if he'd catch a glimpse of her, and sometimes it was the only reason he got out of bed. It wasn't her beauty, and in many ways, he couldn't recall her features when he thought about it, but there was something in her aloofness, in the impos-sibility of it all, that kept him at it.

Manx wondered vaguely about crimes committed by ob-sessed people, idols murdered by their devotees.

The milk bar, dispensing government-subsidized flavored milk and nonalcoholic beverages, was half empty. The reg-ulars sat at their tables, reading papers, playing cards, occa-sionally getting up to spit outside and coming back in. Manx and Freddie told each other about their lives.

"My sister has deliriums. She can't sleep at night. She was really affected by my cousin's death, and all she does is space out in the garden."

"Sometimes it takes a long time to get over a hurt."

Manx blew bubbles in her drink. "I know, that's gross," she apologized. "Anyway, Renu just sits there like a vegetable. I try to snap her out of it, talk to her, get her to play a game, but all she does is sit."

"It must be hard."

"Yeah, well. I guess I've got a better handle on death than she does. Like in first grade, there was a girl in my class who had cancer. We all made her cards, and then she died a month later. I mean, it was awful and everything, but there was nothing you could do about it. I don't think Renu's ever had that kind of experience."

They began to spend their afternoons together, sitting for hours in the milk bar. Freddie had a story for each of the other customers, and his hands flew in the air when he got excited. He told her about growing up in a suburb of New York, taking the bus into the city at ten, getting lost in Central Park. He had abandoned his father's name at some point, and renamed himself Flat for the way it sounded. They agreed that everyone should invent themselves a name. They kept a sharp lookout for Mirazi and once followed her on a shopping expedition, but lost her when she got into a taxi.

It wasn't long before a neighbor reported to the family that Meenakshi was spending a lot of time in the marketplace with a foreigner. Questions were raised, inquiries were made, but when Manx herself was confronted, she smiled sweetly, a rare thing in itself, and said, "His name is Freddie. Let's invite him over."

So Freddie Flat paid a formal call on Nirmila Nivasam. He brought mangoes and cut hibiscus, said *namaste* gravely, and sat in near-silence with Bala and Rukmani. At the end of a half-hour, he rose and said good-bye.

. . .

"Well, he seems harmless enough. And he's so much older than Meena," said Aunt Bala.

Rukmani nodded distractedly. Freddie hadn't seemed very threatening.

"I'm sure there's no harm in Meena spending time with him. I think she misses her father."

Seven

Freddie invited Manx and Renu to dinner. Renu suspected she'd been asked only as chaperon, for Manx couldn't attend alone without tongues flapping. She didn't want to go but with much persuasion she agreed to attend.

"You'll really like him, he's neat," said Manx, ripping the sleeves off a T-shirt.

Renu just made a face and reluctantly stepped into the auto rickshaw. Despite herself, as the motor started and they bolted through the streets, she began to feel an excitement stir within her; she hadn't been out of the family compound since her arrival.

Freddie lived in the French quarter of the city, a section that was part colonial, part hippie in spirit, and generally rundown. Sundays, older British residents gathered on the square to read imported newspapers and wait for the pub to open. Foreigners in mystic robes, their pale scalps rubbed with sandalwood paste, wandered around the ashram and spiritual bookstore. Local college boys frequented the head shops with their African exchange-student girlfriends. A mosque, mysterious as a wrapped gift, was set on the edge of the quarter, and haunting prayers could be heard on the streets. A one-eyed parrot seer set up his box on the square, and although no one believed his fortunes, he was convinced he did better business among the foreigners than elsewhere.

Manx stopped to have her cards read. After spreading the deck out in front of her, the seer took a chained bird from its perch and placed it near the cards. Tottering, the parrot took a few steps forward and nosed a card.

"Little change," said the seer. "Maybe a surprise in a day or so." Then, as if in apology, he shrugged. "These are slow times," he said.

He turned to Renu but she declined. She had more than her share of other-world intervention.

Freddie's apartment was above a tailor's shop that advertised Western-look clothing. Bell-bottoms were still in style, lingering longer than in the West. A Muslim woman, draped in layers of black, stooped over the steps as if in prayer, but she was merely washing the stones. "Please," said a man in rags, holding out his hand as Renu fumbled with coins.

"Hello," said Freddie, opening the door.

"Hi," said Manx.

"Oh," said Renu.

He ushered them inside. Renu studied the room. One wall was painted to depict a sea with a series of asteroids above it, glowing purple and yellow spheres above a blue-green ocean. Ceiling-to-floor bookshelves filled the opposite wall, and others held posters of Jimi Hendrix, someone Renu couldn't recognize, and Shakti. There were plants everywhere, newspapers, and magazines in piles, records stacked haphazardly on the floor, and what looked like a shrine area under a pyramid made of plexiglass. Prisms hung from the window, splaying rainbows onto the floors.

Freddie filled two bowls with vegetable curry and served Renu while Manx dipped a spoon into a jar of peanut butter. Freddie was a lapsed macrobiotic, largely vegetarian, and looked a little like someone who would play a bear in a children's play. He had been a film major at Columbia, a student of Soviet montage.

"Pot had a lot to do with it, though. You could sneak a hit, and let yourself melt into those beautiful shots of grain-fields and sky in Dovzhenko's films. It was pure poetry," he said.

Renu nodded as if she understood.

"Watching movies can have a funny effect on you, though, which is why I hardly go to them anymore. You begin to think that life is episodic, that it contains fade-outs and clo-sure, that if things continue one way, you get a conclusion. The Eastern belief that life is balance without a goal, that you don't have to get anywhere and can hover on *is*, makes more sense."

"But Godzilla movies are good. They always turn out right. Sometimes the scientist wins, sometimes the monster," said Manx.

"Well, they embody such a goofy sense of good and evil. What's great is that the filmmaker doesn't try to pretend it's not a film. It's so fake you never forget where you are, some-thing you don't have in movies a lot," said Freddie.

They talked like this for a while. Renu was surprised at Manx's attention, the way she seemed really to be listen-ing to Freddie, instead of storm-trooping with her words. Once, Bala had asked Renu what Freddie and Manx must find to talk about. "I don't know, probably music and movies," she'd replied. How strange to find that she'd been right.

Sometime in the evening Manx told Freddie that Renu had vision dreams. When pressed to describe her dreams, Renu declined, saying only that she found it hard to sleep at night. She did not want to admit that she was scared of talking about the stone-eaters lest they appear in the windows. Instead, forced to join the conversation, she began to tell them about Alphonsa, her Spanish aunt. From Aunt Bala and the cook, she'd found out bits and pieces of the story and made up what they left out. She didn't know why she wanted to tell the story; she just felt like it.

Freddie and Manx sipped at a joint, and when it was passed to her, Renu coughed at her first draw. Manx smoked at school, she knew, but Renu had never learned how. Clearing her lungs, sitting cross-legged, she began:

One morning in early April, Adda Krishnamurthi, no more than eighteen, took a walk to buy hair ointment. For some weeks, he'd been noticing that his hair was falling out, and was determined to stop the process. At that time, Nirmila Nivasam was smaller than at present, and the carriage house, now boarded up, housed a cream-colored Bentley. A wall still enclosed the house and garden, but in those days a man always stood at the gate, ready with a salute for all who passed through. Now the gate was rusty and left red prints on one's hands. But in Adda's youth, it had gleamed brightly, an effective barrier between the world outside and the one within. On this day that Adda walked whistling a popular film tune, the air was full of dust and the sun lay fingers of heat upon his face.

As he neared the Victoria Fountain, he heard the rattle of wooden wheels. A dark carriage drawn by a set of ribboned horses heaved by. As it passed him, there was the sound of wood being snapped; a shutter was quickly lowered and a white hand emerged to flick a burnt match to the ground. Then it was gone, dust clouds rising in its wake, the hoofbeats barely audible, until it seemed a phantom from another century. Adda stood rooted to the spot as if he'd seen a demon.

On the rare occasion that Bala spoke of it, she would end the story here, and spit out her words. "One white hand," she'd say, "and Adda fell under that woman's spell. Then he left us to marry a foreign woman."

But Renu carried the story further. There was a glamour about her uncle she wanted to crack, a fascination with his story that she didn't entirely understand. Lately, she had begun to connect the empty-handed woman in her dreams with Alphonsa.

Caroline Rightgutter was a woman who preferred the horse-drawn conveyances of an earlier era; eschewing automobiles, she ordered her carriage from London and had it shipped to Pi. She was seventy years old, nearly blind, and possessed flawless arms. According to the local mouths, she was fond of prepubescent native boys, whom she dressed up in silks and invariably named Ganymede, and abandoned after a year or so.

Adda forgot all about his hair, such was the impression of what he'd seen. The sound of wood, the thrust of the arm, the sudden vanishing all teased him so he couldn't sleep. His bed creaked at night, making his mother suspect he was in need of a wife. She decided to bring it up with him at breakfast one day, but before she could broach the subject, Adda surprised everyone by announcing he was off to Europe.

One month later found him dressed in his new Western suit, his leather suitcase packed and repacked on the veranda. His father had thought he meant Oxford or Cambridge when Adda announced his plans, and was humiliated to discover his son meant merely to wander. It was bad enough that a knee injury prevented Adda from joining the services for the impending war in Europe. Troops in India were already being organized, yet

Adda didn't believe any war would take place. Adda's heart was in going. It had to do with Caroline Right-gutter's white arm. To him, it didn't excite sexual fervor as his mother suspected; to him, the arm seemed to symbolize everything rotten in the world. Preserved, perfumed, smooth when it ought to have been wrinkled and sagging—it disgusted him. It represented a power that ought to have been on the wane instead of in full strength. His father thought Adda an idiot and refused to grant him a blessing for good passage. His mother, thin and reedy like a girl, wept and clung to her son, blaming her husband.

Adda traveled by boat to Madras, then took a train across India. He crossed the rice paddies, bright green sprouts poking through clear water, crossed the great plains and mountains. He passed Deccan, Sholapur, Poona, Bombay, Surat, Baroda, and Ahmedabad. Slowly, falling in and out of sleep, making frequent stops at stations that all began to look the same, Adda left his birthright, his family, left a country full of heavy-hipped, purple-lipped women and *paan*-chewing men. From Karachi, he took a train through Iran and Turkey.

"Wait," said Manx.

Renu waited.

"He took a train all the way to Europe? That's impossible."

Renu tried to picture her uncle traveling with nomads, his legs helplessly flapping over a camel's wooly sides. She imagined him swooping about in a biplane, in goggles and a long scarf.

"He traveled on a train," she repeated. It was her story, after all.

At the Basra station, Adda went over to the kiosk to look at titles he couldn't understand, newspapers he couldn't afford. He was reading, discreetly, a cover story in the London *Times* when he felt a tap on his shoulder. He turned to find a tall, dark man who bowed and displayed a translation of a Max Beehan work on Indian sculpture.

"Are you stopping in Baghdad?" asked the man in an accent unfamiliar to Adda.

"I'm going further, sir," replied Adda, flustered to be addressed by a European.

"So am I. I was hoping to run into someone who could help me with some of these names. You're from India?"

The man introduced himself as Giuseppe Lombardo Alvirez, son of an Italian and a Spaniard, an exporter of ivories and an art enthusiast.

"You must be a scholar, you've got that hungry look," said Alvirez.

Adda was embarrassed but not enough to refuse an invitation to tea in the man's first-class compartment. Tea turned out to be wine, and Adda got drunk for the first time in his life.

"What are you doing so far from home?" asked Alvirez.

"I had to leave," said Adda.

"*Had* to?"

"Yes."

"A girl?"

"No, no," said Adda, blushing. He explained to his companion the reasons for his going to Europe, to discover the root of his island's problem. He wanted to know why a man would leave Europe to enslave another country. Drinking through Turkey, Adda grew expansive about his ideas, and detailed the injustices suffered by his countrymen at the hands of the soulless imperialists. Alvirez held that the coming great war would change the world, but Adda could not be sure. To throw off the shackles of two centuries of foreign rule almost required an act of god. The two men found in each other sympathetic listeners, and by the time Alvirez got off in Greece, he had become quite fond of Adda. He implored him to visit Cádiz, and gave him an engraved business card that he'd had made up in Boston. He also left Adda with a bottle of wine to carry him over to Athens. When Adda at last reached his stop, he took his first unsteady step on European soil. He took another and fell to the ground in a stupor.

"Get up, get up."

Adda opened his eyes to find a fat woman in a red kerchief peering at him. She squatted beside him and poked him in the back. This was Theone Apolutes, to whom Adda would send a New Year's greeting card every year until her death by gout in 1953. Theone suggested that Adda try sitting up, and Adda told her he would, but for the enormous weight on his head.

He had missed his stop in Athens, and had arrived at a tiny town called Pyros on the seacoast. Theone took him to her home, a boarding house she owned near the station. She offered him a room. To help pay his rent, Adda fixed things around the house while Theone told him of her life. She had once been an actress, she said, good enough to rival Garbo, but she had quit the stage to marry. As Adda puttered around with an eggbeater, she donned swatches of curtains and recited portions of *Anna Karenina*. After a couple of weeks, knowing all the roles Theone claimed to have played, Adda decided he needed to find work. He thought he could teach English.

"And who will pay a brown man to teach English?" asked Theone.

At the end of two weeks, with all his funds gone and only an ignorant nine-year-old who made faces at him for a pupil, Adda made a momentous decision. He became the first member of his strict Brahmin family to search for manual labor.

He found a job at an olive oil press. The job gave him time to consider what he wanted to do next, although it left him too exhausted to take decisive action. Whether the idea emerged after a period of time, having shaped itself from birth, or simply fountained up in a single moment may be argued, but the fact was that Adda Krishnamurthi of Prospero's Island realized his past eighteen years were nothing if not a preparation for him to become a poet.

At night, his hands greasy with oil, he composed lines in near-sleep, copying them in bound notebooks of cheap paper. In his letters home, he described the foods and clothing, the sea and sky of Pyros, the stars that seemed to drop white-hot and burning into his palms. He sent some of his poems as well. In her letters back, his mother never mentioned the poems. Instead, she wrote about the new well that was being dug in the yard, the death of the elder goat, the upcoming marriage of one Priya Narayan, who "would have made you very happy if things had been different." What she didn't write about was the pain she felt at his absence, how she walked about each day with her hands clutched over her stomach, until it became an accustomed sight; the others of the household would ask, Jaya, how is your pain today, as if it were a toothache or indigestion. She walked like this, while his father would not speak his name.

Adda stayed in Greece for a year, writing poems he gave away to friends. Sometimes at night he'd dream of the white arm and determine to go to England or France, and then one day, he did. After nine years of wandering around Europe, finding what work he could in the shipping yards or factories, hitching rides from traveling soldiers, quartering himself in Paris until the occupation, and later returning after liberation, he found himself in Cádiz, enfolded in the embrace of Giuseppe Alvirez.

"Now we get to the good part," said Manx.

Cádiz is a whitewashed city, so full of the sun's glare that it was "like looking at the house of God," said Alvirez. It faces the sea, and sky and sea compete to present brilliant blues. Alvirez clapped Adda on the back, and proclaimed to have acquired a collection of south Indian bronzes. "Poetry I have little time for, but see—" and here he pointed to a stackful of thin aerogrammes in a drawer, "I've kept your letters, knowing our paths would cross again," he said.

So Adda stayed with Alvirez, occupying one of his sons' rooms. Both of his sons had died in the war, leaving a shrunken father to recover from the fighting. The entire country was trying to reawaken, testing cautiously the newfound peace while aching from the blows received. Soldiers missing a leg or an arm wandered around town in bandages. One day, a man shook his stump of arm at Adda, reminding him of the poor at home.

Adda had been there a fortnight, reading to Alvirez in the evenings, listening to him ruminate about politics and the Americans, when he happened to glance out the window one day. He was stopped by a vision. A girl stooped to draw water from a tap. The arch of her back, her golden hair fixed up in a bun, the delicacy of her neck all burned themselves into his mind. This was

Alphonsa Alvirez, Giuseppe's daughter, lately returned from a stay in Madrid. For the second time in his life, Adda was enraptured by a woman's gesture, but this time, instead of being repulsed, he resolved to marry her.

At first, his love was one-sided, but as Alphonsa began to recognize and later acknowledge his shy smiles and blushes, their courtship began in earnest. Since she was no longer a girl, in fact a few years his senior, she was not constrained by the stern hands that guided girls to silence in the town. She and Adda were free to take long walks, exchange books, and converse deeply. He drew her magic squares, seeking to impress. Smiling, she drew him more complicated configurations, for Alphonsa Alvirez was an accomplished mathematician. "Everything can be reduced to numerical simplicity," she said as they walked through a garden heavy with the scent of aloe and orange. When Adda asked her to marry him and promised to take her to Pi, she thought he meant a metaphor for the transcendental ratio, and immediately agreed.

Alvirez did not seem surprised when they told him, but he raised his eyebrows at his daughter. He had suspected her a more rational creature. "You can't marry here. No citizen would rest knowing a brown man sweeps a white woman into his arms at night. You may have to go to Paris," he warned. But with the confusion of the peace, they found a priest who married them at the border for a fee.

Ten years after he had left, Adda returned to the island, with India rearing up for independence. Bearded, fatter, dressed in an immaculate white suit and silk tie, one of several he'd been presented by Alvirez, Adda stood at the gate of Nirmila Nivasam. Alphonsa, beside him, took one step into the courtyard and fainted.

The old women shook their heads. No good would come of it. To marry out of caste was to stick a tongue out at the gods. The neighborhood was scandalized. Adda's mother had the Spanish bride removed to a cool, darkened room, and when Alphonsa woke after a nap, she handed her new daughter-in-law a cool drink. But such was the look she fixed on Alphonsa, one full of a mother's wrath and loss, that Alphonsa couldn't speak. She lost her voice, and for the rest of her life would speak to no one save her husband and his best friend, Amir.

The early days were hard for her as she examined how Madhupur was like Cádiz but different. One day the sky would be a bright shade as at home, the next day, lighter. She was delighted with the parrots and scared of the cows and water buffalos. She watched intently the village women who carried water on their heads, their backs straight, their hips swaying, their arms held high, and felt ashamed of her own thin body. She translated volumes of Marx and Engels for Amir, and carried small novels everywhere. There were many speeches and marches in those confusing days, and daily riots. Pro-Gandhi and anti-Gandhi factions fought. Amir led raids on army quarters and Adda acted as runner and intelligence officer. The island was shaking itself out of a deep sleep.

Adda and Alphonsa had their private hours, too, their moments of slow discovery. Her fingers gliding through the bathwater to test for hotness, the quiet of his step as he slipped off his sandals. He would buy flowers for her, jasmine buds she fixed to her braid that would bloom by evening and crush dry on her pillow at night.

Renu found it difficult to imagine the rest of it, for something had gone wrong, there had been an end to the bliss.

At first, Alphonsa tried to adapt to the land, but her nervous fingers slipped back and forth over the gap of skin exposed by sari and bodice, that bare midriff representative of a sensuality that strove to live in a country where kissing was forbidden in public. So Alphonsa sat at a spindly Singer, her feet rhythmically rocking the pedal as she fed cloth to the needle's piercing. She made roomy caftans for herself, hiding her body under masses of cloth.

Adda began to work with Amir regularly, acting as party emissary in other towns while Amir tried to raise an army in Madhupur. Adda stayed away for weeks, urging Alphonsa to lend her services to Amir's growing resistance party. Alphonsa was left to make caftans and linger friendless on the veranda. Finally she went away to a Catholic retreat in the hills, writing to Adda of her decision.

Alphonsa was buried by the moon-faced nuns of the Holy Order of St. Magdalene. On the day of her funeral, Adda stood on the steps of the veranda and cut all of his silk ties in half. He never spoke her name again.

"That's all?" asked Manx drowsily. It was all that Renu had figured out. Her throat ached with the effort. Manx had drifted off somewhere in the middle, and Freddie was suppressing a yawn. Renu stood up.

"Thank you for dinner, we really should get going," she said formally. Renu thought of calling around for the car, but the idea of riding in a bicycle rickshaw appealed to her. It was a quiet night and the drivers who had been on strike earlier had settled, and there seemed little chance of rioting in the streets. Freddie closed his palms in a traditional gesture of parting.

A half-rupee starting rate, the driver announced as they climbed in. Bumping along in the rickshaw, Renu watched the gathering dark that began the late night phase of the city's life. Men grouped themselves around kerosene lamps, women peddled hot, roasted chickpeas, and the queues for the cinema stretched out for blocks. A comet streaked across the sky. There was something going on, something marking a new start, a beginning of some kind. But Renu, wary of signs, closed her eyes to it. The motor droned in her head, an unchanging sound.

II

Eight

Nine years ago, Highway Amir, founder of the Free Island Party and general-at-large, proposed a walk to Agnir Bridge. Ever since the road to Madhupur had been built, long before Kish was born, no one had used the bridge much—not only because it was generally inconvenient, but also because it was known to be haunted. But in a celebratory drunkenness, in which Amir imagined himself a lofty and invincible Colossus, the party founder said that his party could defy anything, even spirits. So, at dusk, Amir, Konga the Wasp, and Kish made their way to the bridge.

Highway Amir had established the Free Island Party on Pi as a young man, leading a troupe of men devoted to ousting the English devils from the island. In 1947, when the newly liberated Indian subcontinent declared that Pi must receive independence as well, Amir expected his party to be placed in power. Instead, moderate leaders were elected for the new government, and Amir's party began to disband. Only a few followers remained, outlaws who ardently tried to stir the citizens of Pi to protest. Despite six and a half coups, eleven uprisings, a dozen bomb scares, and numerous civilian strikes, the populace remained indifferent. For a time, Amir was known as the Number One Enemy of Pi, but his danger to the state faded into myth and memory. Some told stories that Amir had panther claws sewn into his knuckles to aid him in hand-to-hand combat; others swore they'd seen him shot seven times and survive. But twenty years after leading a fierce and determined band of renegades, Highway Amir, ex-revolutionary, found himself making umbrellas in the tiny town of Cosu.

One day, when the sun stretched the newly made umbrellas across their frames, Amir woke from a late sleep and discovered a small boy sitting in front of his store. Assuming he was one of the village children turned truant, Amir ignored him. By noon, when Konga strolled over for his daily smoke and gossip, the boy was still there, and when Konga left, long after dinner, the boy had started to make himself a bed under the baobab tree a few yards from the store. Konga reported he'd heard that an old woman had led a child by the hand earlier in the day, but had no idea who they were. In the morning, Amir found the boy again at his door, staring with great pale eyes that seemed to want to eat his face. Nothing could get the boy to speak, so Amir fed him a bit of breakfast, and hoped he'd go away.

"Maybe you're stuck with him," said Konga.

"I'm too old to be stuck with anything, especially a nose-drippy brat."

But after several days, Amir had no choice but to accept responsibility for the child, whom he had begun to call Kish, as no one else wanted him. No one knew anything about the ayah who had accompanied him to the store, and Kish himself was mute on the subject.

Amir first saw Kish as a young recruit for his populist army, and tried to train him in the ways of a subversive.

What he didn't expect was the boy's stubborn resistance to the party. While Amir patiently taught Kish the fifty-three methods of sabotaging a government vehicle, Kish traced the flight of yellow-tipped moths in the air. While Amir recited the glorious deeds of Konga the Wasp and Mani the Mongoose, Kish yawned. He poked at earthworms instead of memorizing battle plans, practiced spitting instead of armament strategies, and always dimpled and smiled an apology when caught. So Amir resigned himself to teaching his newly adopted son to cover umbrellas.

Amir's umbrellas were extraordinary and famous. In fact, to most people, Amir the Revolutionary and Amir the Umbrella Maker were two different souls, a notion that disgusted Amir. His umbrellas were large and colorful, but their charm lay in their handles. Amir carved the wooden handles into amazing shapes resembling flying fish, elegant cranes, panthers, tigers, kingfishers, mongooses, and elephants. He carved a fleet of dancing girls who seemed ready to leap into the rain, an entire orchestra primed for performance, and under a heavy cloth he kept a section of erotic carvings for special customers. Once, Kish came across the secret collection, pulling away the cloth to reveal fantastic men and women; he looked at each one, working to decipher each pose, each twist. Kneeling, standing, on one set of feet, on another, these couples kissed and wrapped arms and legs against grainy breasts and buttocks, and still there were more! He wondered if Amir could have got the proportions right, for it seemed all wrong. On the framework of each umbrella he made, Amir etched, "Free Island Believes in the Liberation of All People."

He taught Kish the different cuts and turns a knife could make, producing a strong slash, flowery whorls. Kish watched as Amir's hands flew over the wood. "One day when I die," he said, "all this will be yours."

"You're not going to die," said Kish.

"Everyone—" began Amir, but Kish's eyes were already wet and blinking.

Now they were on their way to confront a ghost. Amir and Konga walked arm in arm, each holding a bottle of coconut palm wine while Kish trailed along behind them. He wasn't interested in seeing the bridge. He didn't believe in the stories about it, and figured they could all be explained by math and science. At night, when Konga came to dinner and told tales of local ghosts and madmen, like Boona the fat man who dismembered little boys, Kish covered his ears and told himself the times tables.

Now Konga was repeating the story of Godavari, the leper's wife. The leper colony had been on East Cosu for as long as anyone could remember. Although Godavari did not bear terrible scars like her husband's, people kept their distance from her. She was a sweeper, a cleaner of outhouses and stables, a woman whose nose had learned to close itself against the offensive. For years, she crossed Agnir Bridge to do her work.

One storm-cast day, she never made it across the bridge. She stood right in the middle and began to scream. She stood with her hands at her sides and screamed so loudly that all the sleeping babies woke up and began to cry. All the dogs and cats ran around confused, the goats began to jump like crazy and tried to mate with sheep, and the glass window at the Cinema Royale's ticket booth was so weakened it shattered a few days later. For hours the sound went on creating havoc. Rice failed to boil, *puris* didn't puff right, everyone's teeth ached. Pregnant women went into labor early, and only the cows continued to chew grass, indifferent to everything but their food. It was thought that the noise would end by evening, for surely Godavari's lungs would give out, but when she continued to scream past dinnertime, the Chief Minister sent a group to investigate.

There she stood, a mad sweeper woman in a mud-colored sari, hair unbound, screaming with her mouth wide open, her tongue flapping. She began to twirl, and when they came up close, they saw she held a gleaming knife, which she spun to silver flashing. Since there was no way to arrest her peacefully, especially as she seemed to be caught up by an evil spirit, and she already had the taint of leprosy about her, they decided to wait and see. ("A step quite typical of the government," said Amir.) Days passed with the sound heavy in the air, and eventually even the cows lifted their heads with annoyance. An exorcist was called for and again a group made its way to the bridge. But although they could hear the screaming, Godavari was nowhere to be found. The bridge was empty except for moonlight shimmering snakelike on its floor.

The next night the sky turned orange, and smoke filled the air. There was silence. Morning saw the leper colony burned to the ground. The police were dispatched to examine the situation, but in very short time the case was declared closed, the cause of the deaths uncertain. ("The government dogs are capable of anything," said Amir.) But if the town had thought the problem was solved, they were mistaken. Someone ventured near the bridge a few days later; hardly had he taken two steps across before he saw a vision of Godavari. After reporting the sight, he cut his throat. Others saw her in the water, on the banks, forever taunting and always accusing, and the legend of Agnir Bridge was born.

"Well, just let the brazen bitch show herself if she dares," said Konga evilly. Kish tried hard to like Konga, for Amir's sake. Konga was the last of Amir's followers, a captain who had earned the nickname of Wasp because he could squeeze himself into any place easily and quickly. Konga always looked secretive, tricky, forever up to something even when he appeared to be calmly cleaning his fingernails. Now he was singing some nonsense:

Roo, roo, roo
I'm no fool
I'll crow before any cock
Coc-coc-a-roo

Kish hoped no one they knew would pass by. He dragged his feet until he was farther back. He resolved to never become like the two men. He imagined a different life. His best friend Murthi was always talking about making his fortune in America, inviting Kish to come along as a partner. But Kish wanted something else, only he wasn't sure what.

He walked on, ignoring the green growth around him, the bursts of hibiscus like blood wounds. If someone were to have told him that the berries of the gos-gos tree could be ground to cure impotency, or that the five-petal jasmine was once woven daily into the robes of the first rajahs on Pi, he might have been interested. But no one stepped out of the trees, like Robin Hood, to challenge his world. It was all the same as ever.

Agnir Bridge was in sight. Built of closely placed wooden slats, it had thick rope railings, and sighed as it swung in the breeze. The underbrush was tangled and lush at its foot, and above, trees full of monkeys leaned over the bridge. There was still light to see by, although the moon's pale form could be made out in the sky. The sun, fiery red and huge, was clear of pinkish clouds, a lone despot. The water under the bridge looked like liquid fire.

At the bridge, Konga and Amir left off their talk and stared ahead, frozen. Kish came up behind them, disturbed at their silence, and softly drew closer, the long grass tickling his bare knees. Just as he was about to open his mouth to call them, they turned around with a shout, nearly knocking him over with surprise. They laughed hugely at their joke, while Kish turned red.

Embarrassed, he snubbed them, settling down on a grassy spot at a distance. They would probably be here all night, he thought disgustedly. He decided to count leaves. He selected a thin persimmon, rotten fruit lying at its roots. He had a method that worked well: start at the top and go down branch by branch. He saw it as a race, wanting to finish before the sun went down. Amir and Konga sat nearby and sucked at their bottles.

"Divide it into quarters and multiply by four," suggested Konga, but Kish ignored him. He scowled as the monkeys jumped, disturbing his calculations.

Amir and Konga were discussing the old days, disagreeing over who had been in prison longer, who had incited more riots. They reminisced about their last bomb.

"So whose fault was that?" asked Amir, leaning back to belch.

"I didn't assign Mani for delivery," said Konga.

"It was done in good faith."

"All mistakes are."

They had planned to set a bomb in the Chief Minister's office on Independence Day, in order to negotiate the release of three political prisoners. When Amir made the phone call, he said he wanted the answer within the half-hour. For thirty minutes, the government office staff tried frantically to locate the bomb, and after a full hour, Amir had no choice but to push the button. Nothing happened. One of his men telephoned to say it was all quiet at the office, except for a frustrated bomb squad.

"How was I to know that Mani mixed up the date—"

"That he'd think party members got off for the holiday—"

"That he went to visit his mother—"

Listening to them, Kish tried to imagine Amir and Konga as the terrorists they claimed to have been, instead of the buffoons they were now. There were other stories, of ambushes set up for the outlaws by the government, the attempts to capture Amir, the actual shootings, the time Amir watched the head of a fellow member shot off from the shoulders, raining blood. There were days spent in filthy rat-ridden jails, of having a day's rations last an entire week, of sleeping in foul water-filled trenches. But looking at them now, two drunks waiting for a ghost to appear, it seemed impossible to Kish. It was growing dark and he had to stop counting as the trees merged into shapeless shadows.

Konga lit the kerosene lamp that he had brought along. It cast strange shadows on the ground, running lines to the bushes. He and Amir were now discussing another compatriot, Adda Krishnamurthi. Adda and Amir had been childhood friends, classmates always set on one scheme or another. One year, they resolved to find hair-growth oil, a miraculous cure for the world. But Adda had gone off to Europe, and Amir had formed the party.

"Adda was the smartest Brahmin on Pi, and the laziest. It wasn't only to help bald men that he wanted to find hair-growth oil—it was a ticket out of school." Amir looked at Kish. "Boy," he said (he always called Kish "boy" when he was drunk), "boy, if you ever want to get out of this mosquito town, go search for hair-growth oil."

"And sell it?" asked Kish.

"Just find it."

Kish resolved to sell it if he found it and make piles of money.

"Did I ever tell you I once lived in a cave?" asked Amir in the dark.

Kish nodded wearily.

"In a *cave*, boy."

.   .   .

They offered toasts out loud, they pulled open their pants to hold pissing contests, they pelted each other with boastful claims of the glorious days when they were heroes. Drinking further, they laughed loudest at their own jokes, danced with each other in sweaty clutches.

Kish rubbed his eyes and strained to listen to the night in spite of the noise. The monkeys had stopped their chatter and the birds had settled down. Only the frogs filled their throats to cry at the darkness, as the stars cast pale silver on the bridge. Kish wished he were somewhere else, he was already bored with the night. Amir and Konga were fools, idiots, stupid clowns who never did anything. They were cheats, claiming greatness when all they did was eat and drink. He felt hot tears sting his cheeks; he was too old for their stories, too old to believe in ghosts.

The moon flashed silver, spilling a net of light. Then something caught his eye. More silvery than the water or the stars, something glimmered white. Fuzzy, changing, the light skipped in front of him, swayed like a dancer, turned into something else, blurred, floated, stilled, and moved again. Kish stared so hard his eyes hurt, but he felt that even as he watched, he was missing something. He remembered his mother, he saw the light, he forgot what he thought, the light moved. Godavari appeared before him, marked with a face which had seen the horror of life and couldn't stop screaming. *I will not look*, Kish thought.

Turning away, he looked at what was in front of him: the tangled trees; the two prone men; and, farther, the home crowded with umbrellas to be fitted, the piles of handles, spokes, and hooks; the common square fronted by the dozen stores which spread out around Amir's; the shady room where his schoolmaster ruled, as crows, unbothered by Byron, settled themselves on the windowsills; and beyond that, beyond everything, mysterious and inviting, the road parallel to one where he was now, a road fitted with worn stone and beckoning with the promise of the unknown, a road that sliced right into the interior of the island.

Konga was asleep, his body rising in snores, his breath whistling between his teeth. Amir shrugged. He tried to awaken Konga. Seeing Kish, he said, "Maybe he's dreaming of Godavari." Tipping his bottle for one last drop, he scratched his stomach.

"Tie me to a tree!" cried Kish.

Amir stared at the boy, who threw himself at the ex-revolutionary's feet.

"Tie me fast to a tree!" He was ten years old and fighting not to run away.

Nine

It took Kish nine years to leave Cosu. The night that Amir and Konga cradled him in their arms and carried him home from Agnir Bridge, Kish learned the lesson of missed opportunities. If only he had taken off down the road then, stuffed some food in a sock and tied up some coins in a handkerchief. But the two men whispered to him, laughed away his emerging doubts, and dismissed any notion of a world outside the one they knew so well.

Nine years saw Kish grow from a small boy into a lanky youth whose arms and legs seemed not to have met each other. He was quiet, respectful, and attentive to those around him, garnering accolades from the neighborhood. "Such a good boy like Kish is hard to find," mothers told their daughters, biding their time. But Kish lived elsewhere, in a world of danger and excitement, an adventurous place where suffering existed as a veil to be parted with secret words, where truth and evil dwelt side by side in a dragon's lair. In it, he was a hero, a man capable of great change, a person whose even composure was a disguise for the complexities beneath. He was a wild-bird tamer, a woodsman magician, a charioteer with golden bow, a man with a mission. It was a dream of youth, of a boy who yearned for a different life but feared offending his elders. Sensitive to ridicule, he kept his thoughts secret and did not expose himself.

Amir and Konga had come to rely on Kish, to depend on and love him so strongly that Amir could not prevent an occasional ache in his heart. "He'll be going away, and we have to prepare for that eventuality," he'd say to Konga, barely able to suppress his tears at the thought. For it was Amir's dream that Kish attend Engineering College in Madhupur.

He watched over Kish's studies diligently, urging the boy to learn the books by heart. Because, as Amir never tired of pointing out, even though the schools were full of bureaucracy and no one in his right mind would read such a milquetoast as Tennyson twice, a smart man could steal knowledge. Amir came to accept Kish's adamant refusal to become a party leader, but consoled himself with the idea that with a college degree, Kish could do better than umbrellas.

Amir demanded that Kish step away from cloth-cutting duties to read his books after dinner. Kish complained that studying gave his head pain, that the facts mixed themselves up and swam crazily inside him, but Amir was firm.

"That's just your brain exercising," he'd say.

"God damn," muttered Konga, who grew weary of Amir's insistence, "I never went to college and you don't see me the worse for it."

But Amir just rolled his eyes and told Kish that he should get up at dawn to study, for a smart man needed only four hours of sleep. But Kish couldn't sleep. He tossed around thinking about Godavari's face and wondering at its meaning. What had she seen? Why had he turned away just when she seemed about to say something? Certainly she must appear to him again, but the years had passed without even a glimmer of a ghost. Kish thought that in engineering school he'd be no nearer to Godavari, that the austere college walls were sure to keep spirits out. He could not possibly attend.

His best friend Murthi thought he was crazy.

"Are you kidding? Not go to college? Hey, man, you have the easiest chance," he said. "Especially since Snakey's got a flu."

Snakey Sai was Kish's only real competition for the scholarship seat at the Engineering College. Snakey was a small, sleek-headed boy who liked to whistle with abandon. Snakey was also the better scholar. He worked solidly at the books, displaying an understanding that was deep as well as broad. Kish's learning was more glib; he had an agile mind that could absorb lengthy scientific formulas while his real thoughts were on knight errantry. The boys in the class had placed heavy bets on the race.

"What do you want to go for, anyway?" asked Murthi.

"I can't stay here."

"You ought to go to New York—that's where the hot super action is. Man, it's the number one main city, I'm telling you, Kishore."

"I don't have the money."

"That's why you should stay. After you take the exam, you and me will collect on a treasure trove, and man, we will be set. We'll get tickets from my aunt in New Jersey and work for her to pay her back."

"She's not going to send me a ticket."

"So I'll go and work enough to sponsor you. Her ice-cream shop's only the beginning—we can open up a restaurant—Americans will eat anything. And New York's only a half-hour from her house. We'll roll in riches, and we can get everything we need—cars, stereos, televisions as big as a wall, computers, lots of beer, blondes, surfboards, headphones—not cheapo black market junk but the real cola. I mean, they've got a *magazine* called *Money*."

But Kish felt no desire to leave the island; he just wanted to leave town.

"I feel strange all the time, as if any minute something's going to happen, only nothing ever does."

"You shouldn't go anywhere without a plan, Kishore. You'll break the Number One's heart."

"He thinks I'm going anyway."

"So," said Murthi after a silence, "I guess I need to change the odds."

On the eve of the college entrance exam, Kish packed all of his belongings into one of Amir's old dhotis and composed a letter: *I've gone to search for hair-growth oil.* He could hear the rumble of Amir's snores, and quickly propped the note on an unfinished umbrella. Not wanting to risk squeaky steps, and because he felt that this was the way Robin Hood would have done it, he heaved himself through an open window. The night air engulfed him like a heady wine, and he had an immense desire to giggle. Stay calm, he told himself severely, but nothing could stop the wild rush in his heart as he hit the ground running.

Ten

Kish came to a complete stop in the middle of the city square. The bazaars were stalls of noise as shoppers bargained down prices; others headed into giant stores whose windows beckoned with saried mannequins. Young boys held large radios on their shoulders, sashaying their hips to the music. Traffic cops signalled the buses and cars to maneuver past the bullock carts, auto rickshaws, and bicycles while pedestrians clutching briefcases or begging bowls waited to cross the street. One man with masses of curly hair stood like a crane, one leg tucked under, chanting, as a khaki-clad policeman directed traffic around him. Kish looked on with wide eyes.

He felt a push from behind.

"Hey."

"Get moving," said a burly man. "I can't wait all day."

Apologizing, Kish stepped out of the man's way, still watching the parade before him. A group of college girls, eyes made up like movie stars', arms linked together, gigglingly ate mangoes, ignoring the taunts of loitering men. A crow circling above their heads suddenly swooped down to snatch away some fruit, and Kish laughed out loud at the sight. He was in the city, where bird and man fought for food, where everyone raced by with swift strides, where piles of rubbish shared sidewalk with gleaming, several-storied buildings. Smell and sight were overwhelming and Kish gulped it in before letting out another joyful laugh. Madhupur lay before him in urban splendor.

"What, are you laughing at me?"

It was the man who had pushed him earlier. Kish began to explain, when the man punched him hard. Kish fell down but managed to scramble back up, only to be hit somewhere around the shoulder. Kish's fist flew. A policeman made his weary way through the crowd and broke up the fight. In a few minutes, only a quarter-hour after his arrival in Madhupur, Kish found himself arrested.

After several hours, as Kish nursed his aching body, the policeman asked him if he wanted to contact anyone. Kish named Adda Krishnamurthi of Nirmila Nivasam. "Tell him I'm the adopted son of his best friend."

Adda was struck with remembrance as he walked past the row of whitewashed cells. Twenty years ago, he'd put up bail for Amir, who had been arrested in a milk strike. It would have been a harmless event except for Amir's record. The fact that he'd participated in the strike at all still puzzled Adda, for better pay was already under negotiation and Amir's presence hardly needed. Amir wouldn't talk to him as they walked out of the prison courtyard, and Adda thought that his friend was merely embarrassed at such a rash act. Adda remembered how blinding the sun had been that day, his face wet with heat, the surliness of the guard as he let them pass. Two days later, Amir left Madhupur without a word to anyone.

.   .   .

"Like father, like son," said Adda on seeing the sheepish boy
in front of him. Kish began to thank him but Adda cut him
off with questions. After listening to him, Adda smiled.

"You were set up. The goonda probably just wanted some
rice and a bed. Public disorderliness is a common offense,"
said Adda.

"You mean he picked a fight on purpose?"

"It happens."

"He took me for a fool?"

"You were taken."

They were largely silent on their walk back to the house.
There were a great many things Adda wanted to ask Kish,
but he sealed the words inside him. It was a surprise to
discover that Amir had actually adopted a son; he'd never
been much of a family man, so devoted had he been to his
political plans. "Create a better world first, then raise your
children," he'd say. But here was Kish, a grown boy who
struck Adda with such a sense of familiarity, it was unsettling.
He suspected the boy was really Amir's—son of a fisher-
woman, a sister of one of the party members. Amir in his
youth had disdained women, but after settling down in
Cosu—what was he doing in that insect town anyway?—he
must have changed his mind. The child might even have been
conceived in jail, and perhaps that was why Amir had run
away. Adda kept glancing at Kish, still not believing it.

Goddamn Amir. Adda still smarted from the rejection, the
silence that fell between them. He hadn't even returned for
Alphonsa's funeral. He'd been desperate, obsessive about finding Amir that day, asking all the party members he knew,
everyone in the city it seemed. They sought to comfort him,
soothe words out to shield him in his grief, but he brusquely
dismissed their attempts, intent on locating his friend.

For the ceremony itself, some cousin brothers had to grip
his body and force him into the car to drive to the grounds.

It was there he closed his mind to it, letting go of his wife, of his best friend, looking at the people before him. His father had refused to attend, his mother crying as she did all her life. At home, his younger sisters would be clinging to each other, sorry for him, but thinking of their babies. Only Bala had come to him during his crazed search for Amir and said, "Elder brother, you should attend to the duties of a husband." But he had turned from her as well, turned away from all of them, remembering why he'd left the island, finding no comfort in family. It was a charade, how weddings and funerals pulled the family together, camouflage for the lies of blood ties. He turned away from poetry, which seemed only camouflage as well, words merely stirring the unrest inside him, offering no clarity. After his wife's death, Adda discovered what she herself had loved, the cool reliability of numbers, the pure beauty of form and logic. Adda looked at Kish and smiled; this boy, he felt, was not a romantic, either.

Adda ushered Kish into Nirmila Nivasam. Manx was in the garden with Renu, and Adda made introductions.
  "Really?"
  "You were in jail?"
  "Was it crowded?"
  "What was it like?"
  "Will one of you girls get us some tea?"
  "Were you scared?"
  "Were you involved in a college strike or something?"
  "Where is Cosu?"
  "Is it on the river?"
  "Meena, will you run in and get us tea?"
  "You made umbrellas?"
  "What kind of umbrellas?"
  "Did you sell them?"
  "You ran away?"

Adda left them to get the tea himself. Kish was invited to stay, any refusal to be brushed aside. "For the boy brought up by my old friend, I can do no less," said Adda. Kish was telling the girls how he had hitched rides to get to the city, when Adda returned.

"Nothing ever happens to me," said Manx.

The birds were driving Amir crazy. A large roost had settled itself on the baobab tree and sang-screeched for hours.

"I'm going to shoot every goddamn one of them," he said.

Konga walked around the tree to avoid droppings.

"Well, at least I hope he's keeping an eye out for activity," said Amir.

"Activity?"

"Subversive action. Meetings. Unions."

"The island is changing, old man—"

"They can't all be complacent, can they? CAN THEY?" said Amir, his face turning red with anger, then pain. He felt a push on his breast, a sharp push that coincided with a push inside his head. All his life he had devoted to the future, shaping the present only to prepare for the new world, so many hours he'd poured on the boy, his determination to change the way it was around them—all this came to Amir as hammers knocked at him. He gasped, his heart filling with pain, and then lifted his hand to his chest. He began to lunge forward, the pain as sharp as a forgotten assassin's knife.

Konga reached out his arms to catch the falling Amir whose face turned dark. "My god, my general," cried Konga, struggling.

Eleven

Rukmani and Chitra set off for their trip to Ootacamund with a great deal of fuss involving confusion over travel schedules and misplaced tickets, but finally, with the last good-byes waved and final kisses given, the boat set sail. Adda shook his head, muttering about how things never change no matter how much time passes. "They were always scattered," said Aunt Bala.

With their departure, a certain peace settled over the house. Even Renu felt the release from Chitra's incessant inquiries about her health and her mother's never-ending list of pro-spectives. In Ootacamund, they would meet two families with eligible boys, perhaps with an in-law or two in tow on their return. "That way, we can meet the mother and all the chil-dren, see the boy in the midst of his own people. Because, Renu, we want to make very sure of the boy before we go ahead. It is your future we are taking care of, after all," her mother had told her with special tenderness.

Manx refused to believe that Renu was taking the idea of an arranged marriage seriously. "Oh, *right*," she'd said when first told. Her sister, Manx felt, was too smart for this scheme. Manx believed as strongly as her mother that Renu was merely going through a phase; when she snapped out of it, Renu would resist the idea. "Anyway, I won't let her," she told Freddie.

Renu for her part would not talk about it. It didn't matter much to her, one way or the other. She sat in the garden, thinking about her cousin, about her Spanish aunt, flooded and rendered immobile by the volume of thought itself.

Freddie came over frequently in the afternoons, making the house his second home. Renu wondered what it was about island houses that they so readily opened up to strangers, admitting them easily so no one felt ill at ease to drape a leg over another's couch, to rest at someone else's table, to go outside and water the plants unasked, bring in bouquets. Was it American life, or merely her own upbringing that inhibited her from acting as freely as Freddie and Kish, or had it to do with her femaleness? She envied their naturalness, their ease, disquieted on seeing embodied before her what she herself longed for, the unselfconscious movement, the beauty of the casual. She wondered vaguely how different she might have turned out if Bala had raised her; Chitra, she felt, would have been a replica of her own mother.

"Sometimes I think about it, but not so often for it to disturb me. Amir's my father; anyway, he raised me."

"I think I'd go crazy if I didn't know who my real parents were."

"I don't know—some things you live with, not knowing."

Later, Renu regretted her conversation with Kish, and hoped she didn't make him feel bad. Still, it was true: she'd never rest until finding out what was what. The romance of it played with her imagination. His parents could have been anyone, haves or have-nots, kind or cruel. As a child, Renu had wanted to be the daughter of her friends' parents. She liked being around Mrs. Kaminsky, who taught the girls to make cheese blintzes, who stood in front of Carrie's closet telling her to dress more colorfully, that boys notice. She liked Harriet's mom, who drove a sportscar and said divorce was a gift from the heavens. She even liked Lin's mother, who fretted all day about her, who covered her couches in plastic, who called her cat "Smidgins." "But I have nothing in common with those women, Renu," Rukmani would exclaim in bafflement at suggestions of car pools or luncheons. Rukmani's friends were all islanders or Indians, women who giggled for hours over tea and sweets, who disappeared the moment a husband showed up.

As much as the girls disappointed their mother, day after day in America refusing to respect or even acknowledge the old traditions, their mother, too, failed to meet the exacting standards the girls set, the secret hopes of what ultimately are perfected televisual relationships.

Manx took another route. On shopping trips with their parents, endless hours spent in stores with little thought to actual buying, the girls would be dropped off in the pet department, told to behave until they were picked up. Inevitably, Manx at seven or eight would wander away and turn herself over at the cashier's booth as a lost little girl. When her embarrassed parents showed up, Manx was always surprised. She never stopped hoping someone new would come along to claim her.

Kish was almost as surprised by his acceptance into the family as Renu, but supposed it had to do with the bond between Amir and Adda. What he couldn't explain was Bala's attentions to him, warm and sweet as honey scraped off the comb, the way she took him in, asking him questions, seeking his advice on the garden. If pressed, Bala would not have been able to explain her affection; it was just that Kish provoked an odd, motherly stir in her.

Adda played cards with Kish in the evenings.

"Did I tell you how I once traveled on foot to a Moorish palace from Valencia?" asked Adda. "It was a journey of three days and two nights. A couple owning a chicken farm let me sleep one night in their barn, provided I capture a fox for them. I let two chickens die and spent an afternoon building them a new coop."

Kish listened to Adda's tale until he thought he would faint. How much of his life had been spent listening to other people's adventures, other people's triumphs? The wild wind of travel was entering his feet again, rising from his soles to his head, making him long to see what wasn't in front of him. Somewhere on the island was a cache of hair-growth oil and he was going to find it.

Freddie discovered that Mirazi, the Light of the World, had left the island. He had been drinking tea at the usual café, waiting for a glimpse of her Tuesday retinue. Some days, his pattern was so set he forgot the reasons for his actions, and only the lateness of the hour nudged him into remembrance. Where was the Light? When he asked the canteen owner, he was told that she and all her crowd had left for Bombay. "Thirty-four pieces of matching luggage and no explanation for it," the man said, shrugging his shoulders. They had stopped on their way to order takeout.

Freddie felt strangely empty; it was ridiculous, of course, she was an interest, an idle curiosity, what Manx called a fad. But Mirazi gave a certain shape to his days.

He'd come to India for adventure. He wanted to forget about classes, about his parents, about a life too tangled even at eighteen—free himself from the conventions of Western materialism. He dropped out, quit that world of plastic expectations, where his mother was already telling their neighbors about the law schools he might go to. He rejected that, and turned to India, to a different way of seeing. It was what so many were doing, led along by the promise of mystic music and psychedelics, shedding American lives to meld into the East, hoping to pick up grace and salvation on the way.

So he adopted Eastern ways, gave up meat for a while, exchanged his mother's blue-eyed Madonna for a goddess sitting on an open, perfumed lotus. He tried to wear a dhoti, but uncomfortable with unaccustomed exposure, he went back to jeans. On the island, he read no newspapers, aware of scandal and politics but preferring to meditate on the world's events as abstractions of light and dark, good and evil. Once a fledgling member of SDS, he no longer believed in political proselytizing. He thought that he must first flesh out the good and evil in himself, that the outside world could wait.

The girl he'd hung out with for a few years, a long-legged Economics major, had returned to Florida, where she now sold meditation cushions and kimonos. "It's not that bad here," she'd write, but he didn't believe it. Her latest postcard, featuring a palm tree and a pink sky, was taped up to his mirror, where he stood now, trying to find a trace of his father's paunch. Freddie sighed. His life seemed nothing more than a set of mild curiosities, ever the foreign observer, always on the watch. And when something rare did enter his life, he would let it get away. What did Manx say? That people had to be careful or they'd end up in swamps without knowing it. That girl had a word for everything.

Renu got up in the middle of the night. Tiptoeing out of bed, she crouched on the floor and held her breath against the dark. She did not want to get back into bed, fearful of the images that would come to her. She just wanted to get over it. It was not such an awful thing, the dark, she told herself. Even though it wrapped her in whispers. Slowly, she iden- tified every sound she heard; that creak was nothing more

than the loose window, that sigh was Aunt Bala turning in
sleep, that rustle—that rustle—and immediately, without
warning, the heavy handgrip clutched her heart. Her ribs
choked so she had to gasp for breath, where was her breath?
Stop, stop, stop, she told herself, stop, stop, stop, stop, stop.
Her breath was flung from her, and she was on her hands
and feet on the floor—it was only the dark, there was nothing
to fear, but she could not contain the hiccups—stupid, stupid
hiccups. On the floor, on her knees, arms wrapped around
herself tight, she was scared, she'd never been so scared.

She knew dawn was approaching, its light would gently
wade through the house. She felt her stomach harden and
the rise of nausea as she huddled in the dark. She felt as if
she were back in second grade, when her teacher used to
conduct the class single-file to the basement while an air raid
siren whooped. They would practice life preservation with
eyes shut, head down, knees up, breath held, as the scream
of the signal pulsed into their spines. Renu cringed like this
waiting for the night to end.

In the morning, Renu approached Manx.
"I've got to do something," she said.
"What do you mean?" asked Manx.
"If I don't do something, I'll go crazy."

A package arrived by bicycle courier later in the day. Freddie
had come over and was playing Chinese checkers in the
garden with Renu. Manx was imitating famous rock stars for
Kish.
"Now who am I?" asked Manx, screwing up her eyes and
protruding her lips.
"Mick Jagger?"
"Mick Jagger!"
The courier handed over a form to sign, peeled a green

mango while Renu affixed her signature to three separate papers, and rode away. Renu untied the package and shook out a letter.

"It's from Mom and Auntie," announced Renu.

She unfolded a single sheet of paper. Her mother and aunt had crossed their lines, in the manner of eighteenth-century epistles. Renu guessed it had been her mother's idea.

> My Darling Girls, *My Dearest Nieces*, The hill station is lovely *We've had some rain* We are taking many walks *We are sad to think of you* Bala, Adda, Daddy, I send you my love *Bala, Adda, Daddy, I send my love* Don't be a bother to your Auntie *Try to get outside once in a while* Aunt Chitra and I went to a lovely bird sanctuary *Your mother and I try to leave our bungalow every once in a while, although my heart isn't often in it.* I know you are both having fun with your new friends *You must both help each other in your sadness*, I think your auntie is looking very well, *Your mother tries to be cheerful for my sake* . . .

Their mother had sent them two round peacock fans with bright green paper centers. Their aunt had sent Manx a collection of comic books, and for Renu, a string of dried beads, dark brown and wrinkled.

"What is she thinking of, sending you *sānnyasī* beads!" exclaimed Bala when they showed her the gifts.

"Maybe she wants Renu to become a holy woman," said Manx, thumbing through the stack of Richie Riches and Hot Stuffs. "As if I were ten years old," she muttered.

"They're nice, I like them," said Renu.

But Bala was furious and would have thrown them away if Renu hadn't held her off.

"They're my beads, I want to keep them." Renu slipped them over her head and under her shirt, where they lay cold and hard next to her skin.

Twelve

A journey was proposed. A scheme of travel, with train rides and strange buses, roadside eating and much sightseeing was contemplated to brush away the lethargy of a hot, still summer. The possibilities of wide avenues and dirt roads excited Kish, and he wanted to leave at once. He asked Freddie and Manx and Renu to accompany him, his words tumbling out to explain the wonders to be found *there*. They would go to the western coast of the island, past the Malaban forest to Trippi, a town famed for its population of psychics and near-magicians.

Grandfather Das scoffed at the idea. "The entire island is going to sink—what do you want to go shifting balances for?" he asked Manx.

"But you went to Trivandur—"

"Yes, and all it taught me was to remain in my bed. If you knew what's good for you, you'd find a firm, safe place and stay put."

Aunt Bala also objected to the plan. Even to consider her nieces traveling unchaperoned, especially to a place as remote as Trippi, in the heart of tribal country, was lunacy. But Adda was their advocate.

"Come now, Bala-li, they'll be perfectly safe. Everyone travels nowadays, and they'll be with Kish and Freddie. They're modern, able girls," he told his sister.

"Rukmani isn't here to say no to such foolishness so I will say it for her," she said.

"You like Kish well enough, and Freddie is a decent fellow, too. He's read extensively, went to Columbia University in New York City, no small thing, and knows the Vedas quite well. What better chaperon can you ask for?"

"What's to know of the Vedas?"

"You know nothing of them yourself."

"The Vedas won't protect them from the dirty trains—"

"Those girls can't just sit here, shriveling up like old women—they've come all the way from America and they have nothing to do—"

And on they argued, Adda's face getting redder and his sentences shorter, while Bala grew more obstinate, until they weren't arguing about the girls anymore, but about the choices each had made in their lives. Adda caught himself just in time. His nieces were relying on him, after all. So he changed tactics and talked softly to Bala. He recalled to her the many times in the past when their own father had refused to allow them to do things, the resentments it had provoked. He pointed out the benefits of such a trip, emphasizing the educational values as well as the sentimental.

"They will get sick from the food," said Bala.

"They will carry food in their tiffins, and they'll only eat at good hotels."

"They must not stay in any hotels."

"They will stay with my friends. I will give them a list, it won't be a problem."

"They should dress warmly—"

"Bala—"

"Not speak to any strangers—"

"You're—"

"And they must not go for any public bathing."

"They won't even carry swimming suits. They will travel in air-conditioned compartments, they will follow a strict itinerary, they won't encounter ruffians. They will eat at sanitary places, they will keep away from political discussions, and they will say their prayers at night."

"They do not go with my blessings."

"But what exactly will you *see?*" asked Bala later.

"The Antonin Monument, for one," said Manx.

"Well, that place is holy, so you should bring back some *prasad*."

"Oh, Auntie, it's just an old statue," said Manx.

The Antonin Monument had been constructed to commemorate Louis Antonin, who had been Lieutenant Governor of Green Fort, a fortress in Trippi that housed the largest foreign army on Pi. Antonin was a ruthless leader whose cruelty on the battlefield was unyielding until he underwent a remarkable conversion.

During an uprising, five hundred twelve French soldiers and five hundred twelve islanders died, and as Antonin surveyed the bodies with a priest, he had a revelation that might have stemmed from the equality of losses on both sides, or simply from the sight of the carnage before him. Louis Antonin's soul looked at the dead and shuddered a shudder of cosmic proportions. He resigned from his post and joined a Jain monastery, where he remained until he was killed by a milk truck one day. His statue was one of the few that escaped the great monument-smashing of the fifties, because by then, it had gained a reputation. Once, a blind woman had laid down her vegetable basket to rest against the monument. Two minutes after she shut her eyes, she felt a warmth behind her lids. Opening her eyes, she discovered she could see.

Pilgrims began to flock to the monument to touch its healing power.

"I knew a woman who had a steam-burn on her arm that disappeared after she went to the statue," said Bala.

"It's just a war memorial," said Manx.

"Some things are sacred despite themselves."

Thirteen

The Srinath Station, formerly known as the Albert, was an
immense, ornate building with high vaults and thick glass
panels set between tiles painted with neoclassic pastoral images. Like much of the colonial architecture on Pi, it was as
overdecorated as a wedding cake; everywhere, the eye was
assaulted by tumbling cupids and shepherdesses. Modern graffiti tripped across the walls, pale blue skies slashed with de-
mands for the release of political figures.

They were to board the Silver Arrow, once the official
conveyance of the Hilmat rajahs who approved of locomotion.
Renu read a notice that announced the intention of the Madhupur Ladies Club to preserve the Silver Arrow with funds
from a Carnatic concert. Kish hurried her on board.

Wooden-seated, silk-curtained, the train had walls covered
with diminutive rose print, and seats of faded crushed velvet.
Some of the compartments were marked LADIES ONLY or PIPE
SMOKING PERMITTED, while others were infamous for once
housing some of the sharpest games of dice on the island. But
now democracy prevailed among the carriages, and busi-
nessmen sat alongside farmers. Passengers balanced enormous
tiffin cans between their feet, among clothbound bundles and

imported luggage. Mean-mouthed porters heaped abuse on the few stowaways, threatening beatings as well as imprisonment. One farmer's baby methodically wiped her nose on the shoulder of a well-dressed man beside her, while her father smiled. "Say hello to the gentleman," he coaxed while the other snarled and rattled his newspaper. Above all the noise was the steady *datta-datta* of the train wheels going forward.

A man in a neatly pressed suit smiled at Renu, but she ignored him, and turned her gaze to the two nuns asleep against one another. They were oddly comforting in their soft orange saris, their crosses of dull silver. The nuns had already been in the compartment when they boarded, and the man had joined them at the third stop outside the city. Already they'd covered so much distance. Renu found herself wondering about the nuns, what order they belonged to, whether they were roommates at the convent. Was it only the monks who baked bread and took vows of silence? Did nuns make caramels? Somewhere she heard that they made candies for the poor. It must be nice to be a nun, she thought, to be free from the complications and decisions of mind and heart. Renu felt an urge to sit beside these nuns, offer up her hands, ask them to let her walk with them, find sanctuary within their sisterhood. There seemed to be something so safe about it. Perhaps Aunt Chitra was right, perhaps she was fated to become a holy woman.

"Have you ever been to Paris, Freddie?" asked Manx.

"I spent a summer there once," he replied.

"Really? I'd like to go to Paris—wouldn't you like to go to Paris, Renu? I could solve all my life in Paris," said Manx.

"What's so messed up about your life that needs solving?" asked Freddie.

"Excuse me, Miss, but Paris won't solve anything," said the man in the suit. "I went there myself," he continued, "thinking as a youth will, that I would find something there I wasn't finding at home. But Paris is just another park of lost civilization."

"A park?"

"An empty, neglected park, like Europe itself. Its museums are stuffed with treasures from the past, much of it stolen, and its people are old and dying." He placed the tips of his fingers together, and leaned closer. "I found on my return that all I needed was in our India itself, and of course, that includes this island as well. All that we envy of the West, with their ample technology, their impressive productivity, can be had here. My country can provide for my happiness, and what a discovery that was, let me say."

He introduced himself as Nam Singh, an entrepreneur from Bombay on business. "I develop hotels from old hill station houses. Right now, I'm on a V.I.P. project in Faseh which is going to make it the new Agra, the new Miami Beach," he explained.

"Aren't there enough hotels around?" asked Freddie.

"This won't be just a hotel—it will be a super complex. Bigger than the five-stars and the Hyatt in Madhupur, an enclosed environment complete with riding stables, night tennis, and an indoor mall. Already, a famous French designer has agreed to do a boutique with us."

Renu leaned back in her seat, her eyes half-closed and her mind only halfway aware of what was going on beyond her lids. Freddie and Manx and Kish were laughing at something Nam Singh had said, and she thought she could hear the nuns snore. The train's *datta-datta* pulsed ahead; she kept inhaling the dead cigarette odor of the seats, and she was trying hard not to cry. *Datta-datta*. The train passed rice paddies and grassy fields, green hills and small silver lakes; a group of women carrying baskets of rocks on their heads from the quarries; schoolchildren receiving lessons under a baobab tree; a beautiful man, drinking from a coconut, whose bare back made Renu's heart ache even more.

Even as the train moved forward, they could have been standing still; time was that illusory. Progression seemed to have been eliminated. In New York, Renu constantly felt the proddings of the future. All through school she'd been asked, what are you going to do? While other seniors raced to fill out college applications, crafting personal essays full of hyperbole and cramming for entrance exams, Renu left her brochures unopened. She skipped the college fair. She had no idea what to major in, thought vaguely of chemistry. Rajesh was going to be an engineer, and while she could imagine him drawing perfect lines with steel instruments, no such picture appeared of herself. It was possible to be an Undecided, though: three sciences, two arts, and one language were the requirements.

Manx lived for the future, making and changing plans, refusing to settle down to any moment. And although she'd never admit it, it was Manx who believed more in possibility, who had more faith in things to come. Renu moved through the world slowly, so certain was she of its precarious state, that things in it could dissolve at any minute.

"Lunchtime, Renu!"

Who was shouting and why?

Renu opened her eyes to a flurry of activity. The nuns had awakened and were sharing a large hamper of food, Freddie and Nam Singh entered carrying bottles of fake Coke from the station—when had they stopped?—and there was a great deal of talk at once.

"You look famished, my dear," said one of the nuns, handing her a chapati.

Renu silently accepted and pulled a mental veil over herself. Manx, noticing her quiet, asked her if everything was all right, but Renu just nodded. She didn't know how to explain that she was afraid if she opened her mouth, she would start crying and be unable to stop.

Her head was full of tiny explosions and she didn't know where it was all coming from. Where the nuns should have been seated, beaming and glowing in their orange saris, was one of the giantesses from her dreams, smiling and eating and becoming bigger. Renu tried to blink away the image but it was no use. Instead, she listened to Nam Singh's voice, which was filling up the compartment.

Nam Singh had a booming voice, the sound of a man truly delighted with his life, wanting only for others to share his enjoyment. He laughed with his head thrown back at all his own jokes, and leaned forward better to appreciate the witticism of others. Given to conversation, he listed feature after feature of his future hotel, and although he listened intently to arguments opposing his views of free enterprise and economic expansion, he repeated his own beliefs with a stubborn smile, so strong were his convictions. He *believed* in pleasure domes.

"Why not have modern conveniences? Why not luxuriate in exquisitely controlled heat temperatures in a shower massage? Why not have access to sumptuous foods at the touch of a telephone button? Why not create one's own views, mountain or ocean, by your windows? Man is entitled to leisure, and I see little appeal in living in the outbacks," he said.

Freddie's ideas of letting simplicity and self-sufficiency guide the way to a more fulfilling life made no sense to him, for Nam Singh was convinced that happiness was dependent on the present moment. The island's problems, he felt, stemmed from the holy men, the religious reactionaries who wanted to oppress the populace with a set of ancient laws which in turn promoted a lack of interest in technological advancement. All this led to immobility and loss. After all, he asked Manx, what would she do without her transistor? Manx replied quite seriously she would die. Freddie said that the issues were mixed up.

Renu opened her eyes and watched the woman suspiciously. Something was wrong with her smile, she thought as her shoulders and neck tensed up. Something was terribly wrong and something was going to happen.

Something did. There was a tremendous shake, a screech of noise, and the lights went out. The train came to a stop. It had struck a water buffalo.

They joined the crowd at the accident site. A band of villagers had already gathered, several men gesticulating and shouting angrily at the engineer. The dark was an explanation, the train's faulty light had not picked out the shape of the sleeping animal, or had someone simply not been paying attention? It was a disaster, an animal lying dead and a train shaken. It would never have happened in Bombay, Nam Singh muttered. It would take hours for the tracks to be cleared and for the negotiations to begin between the owner of the buffalo and the railroad company. A pear-shaped man bustled about, asking everyone to return to their seats and wait it out. A protest immediately ensued, the air buzzed with words about important meetings, connecting trains, appointments missed, loves lost.

They had halted in the countryside, but a brisk walk could take one to a taxicab eventually, and the taxi could transport one further to Faseh. This is what Nam Singh proposed to his traveling companions, offering accommodations at the soon-to-be-renovated Faseh Palace. From there, they could catch a morning bus to Trippi. Freddie, Manx, and Kish consulted with one another, Renu simply shrugging and saying it didn't matter to her ("Sometimes I want to shake her," said Manx). The three could see nothing wrong with the plan, and it seemed more promising than a lengthy wait on a broken train; the nuns declined the invitation, interested in finding out the consequences of the accident. The owner of the buffalo had in fact promised it to another farmer as part of a dowry, and the two were berating the man in charge of the pen, who insisted with a resigned and unhappy face, since he knew that no matter what happened, he would be the one to suffer certain misery, that the gate had been firmly shut. The mystery was taken up enthusiastically by the passengers, and as Nam Singh led his new friends away, the air throbbed with noisy discourse.

As he predicted, the walk was not difficult; they passed many people headed toward the accident site, holding aloft lamps and torches and cameras. Nam Singh cleared the path with his umbrella, his raincoat tucked under his arm. Renu could not take her eyes off him; she felt as if they were all in a cartoon.

The Faseh Palace was a two-story pink stucco structure with a wraparound white portico. A few peeling wicker tables and chairs were arranged haphazardly on the porch under faded awnings. Thick carved doors embossed with England's lion and unicorn were propped open with bricks, leading to a shallow foyer lined with mildewed books and withered plants. A cat that looked as lively as the interior slept on a windowsill, near some upright croquet mallets. In one corner, an enormous cage contained an aged parrot that Nam Singh claimed had seen the fall of Napoleon.

Two young men wearing pink polo shirts and chinos greeted Nam Singh in the hall, while an elderly man in a spotless dhoti and shirt did not look up from his newspaper at the front desk.

"Any news?" asked Nam Singh.

"No, but it's not the season," replied one of the men.

"It's never the season here," said Nam Singh. "However, once the new place goes up, you'll have to bar the doors, there will be so much business."

The man at the desk let out a snort.

"That's Patel," explained Nam Singh, lowering his voice. "The present owner. Although his sons want to sell, he is sitting on his share like, if you pardon my language, like a man on the pot."

Dusk, peculiar tranquil pause between light and dark, fell slowly in Faseh. The moon, a slim crescent, was faint in the sky, preceding the stars, which would not appear for another hour or so. Renu sat on the porch. Dinner had been a continuation of the conversation on the train, with Nam Singh and Freddie raising their voices and calming down only to get excited again. Patel just glared throughout the meal, addressing his remarks to the parrot. Renu was bored with the argument; there seemed little point in trying to find common ground in what were basically two different viewpoints on life itself. Renu felt that arguing for the sake of arguing was simply an airing of egos, mere verbal wastage.

Night noises sounded from the trees and the forest beyond. She wondered what the place would be like in the morning light. Feeling the effects of the wine she'd drunk at dinner, she yawned. The air, light with jasmine, wisped her hair, tickling her neck. She was struck by another smell, of smoky wood. Renu was reminded of her early years at Nirmila Nivasam where, before the tiles had been laid for the indoor bathroom, a large tub of water would be heated for her in the bathhouse. By the time she'd enter the room, the air would be full of a delicious smoke mixed with steam. She wondered if someone were heating bathwater nearby.

Gazing out into the approaching darkness that would soon drive her inside, she felt a familiar disquiet. Looking up, she saw Rajesh sitting on a porch railing.

Oh, she said, silently. Rajesh glanced at her and then fished a cigarette out of his pocket and lit up. "Oh," repeated Renu, this time aloud. But the word did not act like a spell and Rajesh was still before her. The air seemed to waver the way it can on very hot days. What was she supposed to do?

"I never expected it would be you—" she began. "I thought maybe Grandfather—someone else—"

Rajesh flicked away the butt with his thumbnail, almost angrily, and disappeared. Where he'd sat was only the porch and the dimming outdoor lights. A throat was cleared. She turned around, thinking of what next to say to him. It was Kish.

"I heard you say something," he said.

"No. I mean, it must be the atmosphere—after the train and all," she said. "I don't usually talk to myself."

"You aren't really here, are you?" he said clumsily.

Renu didn't answer. Why didn't he go away?

"I think everything irrational has an explanation," he said, standing where Rajesh had been. "If you look hard enough. There's a story in Cosu that sometimes when you sleep out in the open, a ghost will come and sit on you. Konga used to call them dream-couplings. A lot of people swear it happens. But there is a rational explanation. See, when you fall asleep under a tree, or with your face in your hands, you breathe in a good deal of nitrogen. The loss of oxygen creates a pressure in your chest and you think someone's sitting on you."

Why was he telling her this? "Rajesh was here," Renu finally said.

"Renu—"

"I saw him."

"You're probably just tired."

"I'm not tired, so just leave me alone!" she cried, turning away.

Kish remained in the dark. Maybe she *had* seen something.

Why in the world had he told her about the nitrogen/oxygen theory? Didn't he believe in ghosts, too? Kish wished he could say something to Renu, but immediately he felt embarrassed at the thought. What was he trying to be, an actor in a second-rate Tamil film? No one needed to be saved in this world, there was no reason for heroes. He went back inside. Nam Singh held wide his arms.

"And here," he was saying, "here is where the heated Olympic-sized pool is going to be. Imagine that."

Fourteen

Morning mist rolled onto the hills from the sea, then thinned to reveal a sky going from pink to blue. Their breaths mingled with the steam from their coffee as they waited for the day to warm up. But as they did, it became harder to leave Faseh. The hotel was set on top of a hill, and out beyond the lawns the land dipped into a valley striped with various greens and yellows. Unordered flowers, wild and cultivated, grew everywhere; giant roses spilled from their bushes to the ground, creating a profusion of petals, so that from a height everything appeared speckled and impermanent. It was a forgotten, neglected place, full of a beauty that seduced by its very indifference.

Patel did not seem bothered that no one came to his hotel, that his rooms remained vacant month after month. Every morning, he took a turn around the grounds, inspecting aging beams, unweeded plots, laying his hand upon the land to make sure it was still there. Nam Singh, watching his perambulations, maintained that the place would be swallowed up by the undergrowth and that Patel would be swallowed as well. "Where does he get his money?" Nam Singh would mutter.

The two men never confronted each other directly but existed side by side, wary and competitive. Both were proud of the place and both felt complimented and proprietorial whenever a particularly moving view was appreciated.

The four travelers discovered an old tennis court and were invited to spend the afternoon playing a few sets. It wasn't hard to stretch the afternoon into evening, and there they were, once more at dinner, caught between Nam Singh's exuberance and Patel's restraint. The tension that should have made the atmosphere oppressive was oddly absent, possibly, they reasoned, because the animosities between the two men were so clearly defined and set into such familiar patterns that it was simple to ignore. After dinner, Patel motioned his hand toward one of his sons and the latter wearily left the room. He returned bearing a tray set with glasses and a dusty bottle of armagnac, a black market coup. A glass was offered to Nam Singh, who declined, but, when Freddie nodded, Patel frowned so severely, and asked if he were certain, that Freddie quickly changed his mind. His duty done, Patel signalled his son, and the bottle, as it must have been countless times, was safely whisked away.

Lotus eaters, they lingered in Faseh. Every morning they would rise, vaguely planning on leaving, but their hosts would press them to stay a little longer. New amusements were found, an abandoned aviary, a shuffleboard, a Victrola and Cole Porter records. Freddie and Manx and Nam Singh smoked away hours with marijuana in the hills. At first, Nam Singh was intimidated by Manx's frank manner, but as the drug and afternoons wore on, he became more confident. "You must have been very free in America," he told her once.

It was Kish who finally realized they had to leave this Xanadu. Out there was a world he longed to explore, and surely they'd lost too much time lingering. He persuaded the others and soon they were bidding good-bye to Nam Singh and Patel. Nam Singh plied them with rugs and blankets, on the chance they might have to stay at inferior hotels with lumpy beds. They stuffed food in their packs and again refused the cab he wanted to fetch for them. At last, Nam Singh heartily shook their hands American style and told them to return soon.

"Of course, you might not recognize the place," he promised cheerfully.

It was a perfect day for walking, the kind when merely moving your feet could cause your heart to soar. There was no need for words. And when a gentle rain began, softly misting their skin and creating droplets in their hair, it lasted only minutes, just enough to transform everything. Rainbows—which poem read *rainbow, rainbow, rainbow?* Renu tried to remember but couldn't—shimmered on their path. They passed few people, a herder, a trio of schoolboys. They took off their shoes to sink their feet into the earth, unbuttoned shirts. Kish felt he could be an animal, walk on all fours and push his face into the grass, that if he wanted to, he could spin his tail and clamber away into the trees.

They came across a magnificent tree that no one could identify. Its trunk twisted and bulged and broke into an array of branches from which thousands of leaves gleamed like iridescent beetle wings. Freddie saw it first and stood gazing at it, waiting for the others to catch up. Renu was reminded of another tree in her childhood, where she used empty coconut shells for teacups, where she'd sit for hours and refuse to come back inside the house. When Kish saw the tree, he saw better trees ahead, and urged them to keep walking, keep going. Manx, intent on remembering the words to a song, did not see the tree.

The bus painted on the sign looked like a rhinoceros. Neither animal nor vehicle was in sight. It wasn't really a bus station, only a place with a sign and a schedule plastered on a post covered with graffiti. FREE THE 10,000. Which ten thousand, wondered Renu; were they from the present or the past? Were they on the island or in the Middle East? Somewhere, ten thousand were suffering, screaming, and the connection between them and the world she inhabited was crucial, Renu knew, but she couldn't see it clearly. She felt horribly magnanimous as only an introverted nineteen-year-old can, wanting to whisper, yes, I share in your pain, I suffer what you suffer as well.

"Nam Singh was right—the schedule's right here," said Kish.

"And we missed our bus anyhow," said Freddie.

Since another bus wouldn't be coming until morning, they decided to keep on walking along its general route. The idea of turning back was disheartening, and having come to the crossroads and continuing on past it was exhilarating in its own way.

By the time night fell, it seemed natural to camp out. The night was so warm, the grass inviting, and they appeared to be miles away from any town or village.

"Do you sleep outside a lot?"

"I used to. When I first came out here, there'd be huge campgrounds for us expatriates, outdoor parties, really. There was this woman, a Ringo fan, who used to paint her nails, fingers and toes, every night. I couldn't sleep for the Revlon Purple Passion in the air—it drove me crazy—I hated the smell."

"She probably waved her hands—you don't *really* have to do that."

"Once my friend Mike and I decided to set up camp on the Madras beach, a very secluded part we thought. In half an hour, a dozen people were standing around, staring at our tent. It was incredible. We didn't know what to do so we thought we'd demonstrate how it was put up. We must have looked like half-assed nitwits. Finally, a reporter from *The Hindu* showed up and started taking pictures."

"Were you in the newspaper?"

"The tent was. We gave the photographer an L. L. Bean catalog."

"Maybe he ordered something from it?"

"Do they ship overseas?"

"Yeah, I don't know, but Freddie, did you ever meet Yoko? I would love to meet Yoko."

"Murthi and I used to sleep outdoors sometimes. We'd pretend we were aliens from another planet."

"We weren't allowed to go to sleep-away camp."

"Mom used to be so hyper about it—like we'd catch diseases or get lost or something."

"It was just something she had never done herself."

"And plus we were girls."

"And maybe boys and apes would swing in through the trees."

They lit a fire. They laid down and slept.

Manx woke up. Kish and Renu were breathing soundly next to her. On her left, Freddie was sitting up. Manx crawled over.

"Why aren't you sleeping?"

"I'm keeping an eye out for goondas."

"Oh. Are you thinking about Mirazi?"

"No. Yes. I don't know. Where do you think she is?"

"Not in Bombay?"

"No."

Manx watched Freddie. His lashes were light, light brown. He looked much younger than he was, even though his hair was thinning, exposing a wide forehead. Manx watched Freddie and could not think of anything to say. She touched his forehead with two fingers, tracing the lines. She kissed him.

"No," he murmured, "I never met Yoko."

Renu dreamed of the three women. They were painting their nails, then tapping them on smooth round rocks. They closed their fingers around the rocks but instead of drawing them to their mouths, they were throwing them at her. She was being pelted by rocks and she put up her hands to protect herself. The three women flicked stones at her with their newly painted hands, and then they were flying, their bodies pointed toward her, swooping down on her—Renu woke up. Panting hard, she stared into the dark, trying to remember where she was. Renu looked for Manx, but saw her sister and Freddie embracing. Quickly, she looked away, but looked again to make sure. She closed her eyes and concentrated hard on a sleep-inducing mantra.

Kish was the only one who slept through the night. He dreamed that two large faces were staring at him and that he was a baby. He was trying to make them smile, and stuck his toes into his mouth. He touched his baby penis, and finally someone lifted him up, but instead of letting him rest at her milky breast, he was passed from hand to hand until he became something else. He spent the rest of the dream trying to figure out what he'd turned into, but the answer eluded him.

Just before dawn, four members of a local fisher tribe came upon the travelers. After a brief consultation among themselves, they decided to let them lie; it was near a harvest festival and they were on their way to escort their sister's bridegroom from a neighboring tribe, the occasion too auspicious to risk tangling with unknowns. Had they known that an island girl slept side by side a white man under a blanket, they would have killed them all on the spot.

When Renu woke up again, she saw a large monkey sitting on its haunches, idly scratching itself. For a moment, the creature's eyes locked onto her own, and she was uncomfortably aware of its powerful hands, its strong jaw, its teeth as it pulled back its lips. But just before she cried out, the monkey left of its own volition.

Despite herself, Renu felt shy toward Manx and Freddie the next morning. She couldn't meet their eyes and didn't know what to think. Manx was a child, fifteen, a baby, *her sister.* But there she was, beaming a kind of happiness that strove to adjust to teenage cool, making for a girl who was a little bubbly, a little smug, a little nervous, and more than a little determined to prove that nothing had really changed. Freddie for his part was quiet, and perhaps in response to Renu's discomfort, solicitous toward her. Renu wondered if Kish knew, if he could tell. She wondered if Kish had ever slept with a girl. Suddenly, she felt so depressingly inexperienced.

"KAMPO-MUNDI PARTY ADVOCATES MAHALA-PREEM FOR DISTRICT SUPERVISOR. A MAN WITH A DREAM AND THE MEANS."
A blast of noise shook the pastoral quiet. A white truck with speakers mounted on its roof approached the travelers. Its driver was a fuzzy-chinned man, cheeks bulging with betel, who had a dreamy expression on his face. They flagged him down and inquired about the next bus. He stared at them as if he spoke neither Tamil nor English, but then

jerked a thumb behind his ear. They looked in the direction he indicated. The road lay still except for the dust engaged by his truck. Then a fat, red double-decker bus appeared, mirage-like, on the horizon, making its bumpy way toward them.

Renu leaned her head against the window and there was Rajesh doing cartwheels in the fields.

Fifteen

Trippi emerged as an oasis between green mountains. The road dipped steeply down, roller-coaster style, leading to the town in the center. They entered late at night, when neon signs winked conspiratorially at the busload. There was one long main street and it seemed that the entire town was out on it. Stores were jammed tight next to movie houses next to exotic restaurants ("Authentic Dixie Food" claimed one) next to billiard halls next to more stores. Cafés spilled chairs and tables onto the sidewalk, umbrellas sporting lace and fringe glittered with tiny electrical lights. Trippi was a dream, a real estate scheme thought up by a group known as the H Collective, who bought out the main heart of the town and turned it into an all-day, all-night carnival. It was a notorious place, untouched by the dry state laws, a haven for philanderers and hedonists, escape artists and the blessed. It drummed energy and heat on its dirty sidewalks, and stirred up the feet of all who chanced to walk there.

"What are we going to do here?" wondered Renu as the bus pulled to a stop, and a dozen taxi and rickshaw drivers pounded on the windows, offering their services. They decided because of the late hour not to bother Adda's friend who would have put them up for the night. But finding a hotel was difficult, as a university-sponsored Colloquium on the Little i and the Flight of Numbers was taking place, and nearly all rooms were taken. At last, they found a room that contained some mattresses on the floor, a basin that contained no water, and a window that flashed green, then red from a sign directly above advertising imported cigars. Travel-worn and exhausted from sitting, they fell asleep, unaware of the roaches, lizards, spiders, the lone nocturnal scuttler that poked its furry nose in search of food. Had she known of their lodgings, Aunt Bala would have fallen like a domino.

By morning, the town still hadn't settled down. The streets were crowded, an electric buzz remained in the air. Manx leaned far out the window and caught a glimpse of a naked couple standing back to back in the opposite window. She waited for them to do something, but they remained perfectly still. She drew back in, exhilarated. She was fifteen, on the road, capable of anything.

"Let's go out and eat a monster breakfast," she said. "I'm so hungry, I could eat three breakfasts."

They found a place that served *dosas* and eggs, and ordered screwdrivers because someone had one at the next table and it looked delicious. A dozen languages rose in varying cadences all around them, and Renu imagined they were overhearing high-voltage drug deals and arms trade arrangements. Everyone looked like a spy.

They roamed the streets. There was so much to look at all at once. Men with brilliantly colored mustaches balanced parrots and mongooses on their shoulders. Women in glitter and feathery costumes strolled arm in arm, lingered at shop windows, adjusted a sandal strap. Prostitutes, eyeing customers from a brothel balcony, threw down roses at passersby. Someone hurried along in a trench coat and dark glasses; she stopped and peered at Freddie who was startled to recognize

Mirazi, the Light of the World. She disappeared before he could speak.

Renu wondered if they would see a man in a gorilla suit, and two minutes later, there he was, shaking his head free from a furry mask. "This is worse than Vegas," they heard him mutter.

She struggled to keep her eyes focused in front of her. There were so many people, she didn't want to get lost in the swell of bodies, and she held onto Manx's—or was it Freddie's?—hand. She was getting dizzy. Someone poked her. She turned around but there was no one there. Then someone grabbed her arm and she looked to see Rajesh.

"You're having a great time," he accused.

"Let go."

He vanished. She hadn't felt his hand; there had been only a suggestion of hot air, a sensation of pressure on her arm.

"Come back," she said.

"What?" asked Kish.

"Nothing."

Sometime in the afternoon, they tasted champagne, but found it was a watery Estonian import. "But it looks like a liquid jewel," said Manx, which struck all of them as a fairly profound statement.

"I can't believe she's here," said Freddie for the fourth time. "What do you think she's doing here?"

"Maybe she's a spy," suggested Manx.

"Selling secrets to the superpowers," said Kish.

"Double-crossing the Communists."

"Maybe she's on a mission from Mars."

"Yeah, maybe she's a Martian."

There was something about the sign. It proclaimed in neat green lettering, MARYA THE SEER. Underneath was a picture of an eye on top of a pyramid, like in American money. But the eye had a mind of its own. It moved. It winked, peered left, vanished into white. How could they resist?

Marya the Seer was poised like a harpy in her purple sari, hunched on ancient knees, balancing a bowl in her ancient hands. She chewed lotus root, swirled the tea in her bowl before drinking, and waited for customers. It was rumored she turned into a winged creature and roosted in a tree, for no one saw her after sundown, and her tent was always empty at night. Her hair was red, streaked with white.

"I take only one person at a time," she snapped when she saw them, "and I only have room for one today."

They conferred a while, barely suppressing giggles, until three of them withdrew, leaving the older girl who, without her companions, became shy.

"Sit down," said Marya, inspecting her fingernails. They curled five inches long on one hand.

Renu looked around herself nervously. Amid soft cloths draped like canopies overhead in the tent there were dried peppers and flowers hung upside down, and an electric Mickey Mouse clock that told time with gloved hands. She stared at the seer, who was silent and rocking.

"I see the dead," blurted out Renu.

The seer did not seem impressed.

Renu breathlessly continued, feeling less and less sure of her words as she went on, but unable to stop. She told the seer the circumstances of Rajesh's death, the predictions for her own demise, the way her dreams tormented her.

"What do you want?"

"I don't want to—to be affected. I want everyone to leave me alone. I want to be alone."

"By yourself?"

"I want solitude, the way the holy women in the stories had it." Here Renu imagined the quiet, ordered ways of a life in the woods or in the mountains, the calmness of it, the purity.

"It's not really like that, so calm and pure," said the seer. She ignored Renu's surprise. "What do you know of solitude? Do you know what it is?"

Renu shrugged. The seer sounded like an aunt.

"Do you think solitude would release you from your cousin?"

"I don't want to be 'released' from Rajesh, I just want everyone to—to—I don't know," she said, miserable.

"And what of your power?"

"I don't have any power."

"Your visions? Your dreams?"

Renu didn't answer.

"Do you know how I came to be a seer?" asked Marya, leaning forward suddenly. "Any kid can have vision dreams, it's not such a great thing. But few can focus their sight and increase their power. Few see the truth beyond the truth. Do you think you have the capacity?"

"All I have are nightmares."

Marya lifted her heavy lids to look past Renu, seeing herself as a girl. She rested the snake of the pipe coil in her lap and felt a familiar stirring within her. Yes, she needed to see it again, needed to take the past and frame it with words. Her customers thought they sought magic predictions when all they really looked for was example. Sometimes the recognition of the familiar was so startling it was mistaken for vision.

"Let me tell you how I became a celibate," said Marya, beginning. "Let me tell you why I refuse the world of love interaction.

"At the age you are now, my body had reached its most perfect self. My skin was smooth, my hair fell like silk to my calves. I luxuriated in the senses of my body, felt proud of what it could do. I knew the pleasure of a husband to whom I was devoted, thoughts of whom filled my mind every day, whose numerous tiny gestures kept me in a perpetual blush. Never had I a moment he was not a part of. But then I discovered even as I was deeply immersed in my love of him, even as I braided my hair thinking of his sighs, that his devotion to me was not as singular as mine was to him. Astonished, I confronted him.

" 'Is it true,' I said to my love, 'that you took to bed Gita the milkmaid, and the fishmonger's daughter, and wife of the District Deputy of Cosu?'

" 'Yes,' he said, smiling at me.

" 'And the sister of our neighbor Rajeev, and the Bupta twins, and Rajeev himself?'

"He nodded, picking flowers.

" 'That you toyed with the affections of Gopal the cinema usher, Sumitra the film actress, as well as the couple who own the entire Star Sapphire movie complex?'

"He grinned as if to congratulate my perception and handed me the roses. I must tell you he was quite shocked when I asked him how he could possibly love so many and live with me.

" 'But I think of you all the time,' he said. 'Like Krishna and Radha.'

"Krishna! Krishna our fine Lord who professes love to Radha, only to love a thousand girls at once; Krishna whom each girl believes is her own true love; Krishna who steals the gopis' clothes and stares at their nakedness unabashed, whose mouth wouldn't let butter melt, who is always forgiven. For who can see a picture of our Lord and not smile back at his sweet smile, the soft blue curve of his cheek, his dancing tiptoe step? Krishna!

"It was not Krishna I cried out to in my pain, but the Mother Goddess, asking her why she rained such iniquities on me, her devoted servant. I shut my eyes to my husband, whose eyes filled with tears, the very eyes I knew so well. I went to the temple, took cold baths, walked on brambles to gather roots for my supper, slept on stone. After months of such severity, I realized all I truly wanted was to impress my love so he would renounce all the others and save his attentions for me alone. And in that moment, I realized the futility of such a hope. So I began to change.

"I began to shed every part of me that desired a connection with others. I closed my open heart which made for allowances and forgives, which admits one man's foot and his hunger. I rid myself of the trust, the uninhibition, the generosity of spirit that real love subsists on. I closed my open mind which sought attention from others, which needed an audience to display its brilliance.

"Do you seek lessons? Here are my instructions for solitude. You take all the channels that man and woman allow to be built between themselves, and you begin to seal them off. You take a freezing gun and you start to shield yourself. You point it in the direction of your heart, your mind, and let it stream slowly, no room for contradiction, no room for second thoughts. You slacken your face until only the smile of the beatific, a simple, gentle line of mouth appears, for you have become unbothered, unconcerned. Your eyes are no longer focused on this earth but beyond.

"You find a small space, a room, a cave, a hole, and you clean it, free it of debris as you have freed yourself. You light one light and you sit. You are celibate, untouched, near holy. You have emptied yourself of passion, emotion, opinion. You leave your body. You can have a certain peace."

Marya dragged so deeply from her pipe it appeared she might pass out. Renu was swaying, and she saw the seer's words as separate, alive creatures, stalking her mind. The room seemed to be spinning, everything out of kilter, and she imagined she was flying.

"But there are practical considerations," continued Marya.

"In our society, how far can an unattached female get? She cannot remain ordinary, if she wants to be unbothered and free. So I became Marya the Seer.

"You see, in this life, women are constantly asked to become brides. You can be the bride of a man, of another woman, of your parent, of a teacher, or a god. You can marry the past. Whose bride are you, Renu?"

But before Renu could answer, the seer spoke again.

"You want to free yourself from grief and channel the force of your mourning, flee from your sorrow. You cannot do that. You can only let the tide of emotion sweep over you until you lie exhausted at the shore. You will want to sleep for days, and when you wake up, rested finally, you will see relief on the faces of everyone around you. They will think, ah, our darling girl is back, but nothing will have changed. The dead will remain dead."

The seer looked at Renu with impassive eyes and sucked at her nails.

"Tell me," she asked, "why are you stuck with the memory of the dead, this necrophilia?"

"Rajesh is my twin."

"But he doesn't exist as he was, only as you have created him."

"No, no, no, it's not like that at all. He was my twin. Having a twin is special. Somehow you know that there's someone who is like you, someone doing what you're doing, maybe not at the same time, but there nevertheless. It's like Rajesh could live for me and I for him, only we didn't have to be together, but we were connected by an invisible string." Renu paused. "You wouldn't understand."

"I understand that each one of us can be our own light. We can even be The Light of the World. We all have our disguises and nothing is what it seems. Anyone who wears sunglasses can look like a movie star. But we each make a choice of life. I chose to leave my husband and nearly died of neglect, but then I made a choice of life. Not everyone will agree that it was a good choice, but I chose my light."

"Your life?"

But the seer didn't correct her, merely stared away. "Your life is your life," she said.

"What?"

"Your life is your life."

"Anyone can tell me that."

"I'm saying that reconstruction is possible. It's not outside the realm of reality. You can change yourself and anyone who tells you different has given up. But it requires enormous discipline and imagination. The change occurs inside. You cannot change the world around you, you can only determine your own path."

"Isn't that, well, contradictory to your profession?"

"I deal in circumstances and suggestions. I can tell you how the moon might affect your action, the magnetic pull the planets play in your life, but I cannot tell you your life. Your life is your light."

When Renu stumbled out of the tent, the others were waiting for her.

"Well?"

"Well what? She didn't say anything," said Renu.

They didn't ask further. But the eye on the sign followed them as they walked away.

Sixteen

From the seer's tent they walked further into the city, amid shapes and colors that were buildings and landmarks in one glance, and fantastical props for a visionary film in another. They stopped again at a tea shop, ate, drank, and looked some more. Renu was so obviously keeping her distance from the others that finally Freddie, the most tolerant among them, had to say something.

"Renu, are you upset because you're grieving, or because you've forgotten how else to be?"

"What do you mean?"

Freddie hesitated before answering, but Renu, suddenly furious, rose from the table.

"What would you know about it, anyway?" she cried. What did he know, smug white male American, comfortable and born to a life of ease, someone who could never understand. All of them struck her as absurd, unfeeling, fake creatures, incapable of real emotion. They had nothing as big in their lives as she had in hers, and they would never, she thought, angered and stung, *never* understand the complexities of the feelings she possessed. She drew her virtue around herself like a long, thick, dramatic shawl and drained her glass.

Blinded by tiny tears, her hair sticking out all over the place, she left the table and walked until she could no longer see, lost in a surging crowd.

She found herself in a side alley. A group of men lounged against the wall, brown island males, young boys with no work, dressed in fancy frayed long collars, skintight jersey printed shirts. Menacing men who looked like they raped women frequently. Her upbringing made her seek out another female in the area, some woman, to give her safety. Finding none, she retreated. There was sunlight once again, familiar shops, tourists, and her own table. Sheepishly, she returned.

As the afternoon lit everything with gold, making pinpoints of color when they shut their eyes, they found themselves in front of the reliefs of Shipra. In the thirteenth century, a fortress was built in Trippi to guard the city from an invading army of Moguls. The fortress was easily overtaken, and the city would have remained under Mogul rule had not the commander Buqua'ar Al-duhr contracted an inexplicable illness in which he lost the mobility of his legs. The army withdrew, and the city was left with a destroyed fortress and only half of the North Wall standing. It was while clearing this wall that fragments of another building were discovered, a temple dedicated to a local goddess.

The find would have been unremarkable except for a curious set of reliefs, a depiction of men, women, various beasts, and children all crowded together on the stone. All the figures were in the throes of extreme emotion, their faces etched with bulging eyes and shocked mouths, limbs askew in horrible directions. Nails or rays seemed to be piercing or emitting from their ankles and wrists, from a few heads. The animals, horned, snouted, three- and four-footed, were on their backs or sides, caught in frenzied movement.

The Great War over the Shipra Reliefs was a topical concern in academia. The University of Bombay's archeology department held that the reliefs were portraits of pain, that the stone carvers were trying to show the horror of war or plague, while the Research Institute of Hyderabad maintained that spiritual passion led its disciples into contortions of body and mind, that the depicted were no less than angels in ecstasy.

The reliefs were cordoned off with light chain fencing, fixed with spotlights to facilitate nighttime viewing, and offered to the public to make up its own mind.

"It's so elaborate."

"It's so weird."

The others began to debate among themselves on the possible sources, but Renu was unable to join in. If she looked at them one way, it seemed to say passion; if another, torture. The reliefs were compelling and the more she stared at them, the more they lost their meaning, emerging as soft risings of stone from stone, here an upturned elbow, here a foot, bodies levitating from the wall without context. Hypnotized, she had an idea that if she could only get close enough, right up to the figures until she became one of them, if she could imitate their movements, perhaps then she could understand their motivation. It seemed important that this one thing not escape her knowledge, that she exercise her mind somehow.

Gently the others gathered her from the wall after she'd crossed the fence and hugged the figures with her palms and face.

They went to a large canteen for dinner, a cavernous place filled with long tables and benches, equipped to serve an army. Two dinners were offered, "North style" and "South style"; within minutes of ordering, waiters arrived bearing trays of steaming rice and breads, ladling *sambar* from vats on wheels.

Myriad mouths chewing and swallowing filled the room. On the back stairs, children gathered to wait for the scraps.

They were unseen and unheard by the diners, who, after their meal, would confront a chorus of pleas, and depending on things that had nothing to do with the actuality of poverty, but whether the just-finished meal was satisfactory, whether a boss had been rude or complimentary, coins would be flung or withheld.

That evening, Manx was violently ill. Clutching the basin, her stomach heaving, every limb exploding—she was certain she was going to die—Manx was sick as she'd never been before. All the drinking, all the food, everything emptied out of her, and as soon as she thought she was finished, her stomach erupted again. Freddie berated himself for not being more observant as he cleaned up after her. It was a long night, and Renu finally convinced the other two as they put Manx to bed that they should get some air, that she and her sister would be fine.

So Freddie and Kish headed for the hotel veranda while Renu sat with her sister, smoothing her damp forehead. Manx's hair was getting longish, and she now resembled a waif, a brown elf temporarily alighting on the earth. She looked peaceful in sleep, and Renu knew that tomorrow she would be better and ready to drink again, somehow triumphant from having survived a bad experience. Her sister was eager for scars.

Renu wondered about Freddie and Manx. He was such an unlikely figure; at home, Manx fell for androgynous blonds who affected disaffection, tattoo-tough singers who mouthed violence on television. Manx had laughed at Renu's own favorite rock stars who wore bell-bottoms; times are changing, she'd say. And now Freddie.

Manx had never had Renu's shy hesitancy about the other sex, never tunneling her words in anticipation of what they might say. Who *cares* what they say, no one's going to remember anything, Manx would insist, tossing her head, on her way to trade tapes or play war games. Renu sometimes wondered if she and Manx were truly related.

Renu was restrained, fussed too much over her mother's codes, and as a result had gone into agony when Billy Bailey asked her to the prom and she couldn't just come out and tell him why she couldn't attend. She couldn't imagine the scene if a squeaky-clean, blue-tuxedoed, corsage-carrying Billy arrived at their door, and she was afraid to try. Easier to avoid him, avoid her friends, mumble excuses, and pray for graduation to come quickly. Easier to daydream about Rajesh, who (she suspected) would have automatic approval from her family.

Freddie was nice, but she couldn't imagine having a sustained conversation with him, he seemed so distracted sometimes. Still, he had made an effort to talk to her that afternoon, and she'd pushed him away. Every day, Renu thought she was over it, that she could go back and be the Renu everyone remembered, that she herself knew. But somehow she only felt she was sinking deeper, that there was no leverage. She wanted to wake up, face the dawn as if it were an expansive, clean plane, veils removed, clouds cleared, and let her life flow back to her. But each day was deceptive; it would start off fine, but suddenly the boom would lower, unseen, unlooked for. Anything could trigger it, a gesture, a turn of mouth, a fallen cup. And the dark mood she'd come to loathe would fall over her quickly. The seer had said there was no way to channel it, that she would just be unhappy. But Renu felt the seer was wrong, that there was a key, a method, only she just hadn't found it.

Renu watched her sister sleep, her little girl's face slack and tender. It hardly seemed possible that Manx's body had shook so, spasmed with pain. Funny, too, how all that drinking hadn't affected *her*, even though she must have had as much as Manx. All she had was a dull headache; there had been no release.

Seventeen

They stayed in Trippi for a week. They wandered the streets and took in the sights, as vacationers, as tourists, as visitors, until the city began to seem too familiar, and they were no longer diverted by its charms. Still they walked around doggedly, seeking better diversion, better delight. Tourists can wear down any city and Trippi, whose existence depended on tourism, protected itself by indifference. It offered what it had, knowing that it was only a matter of time before it could shake the visitors off, wearily and easily as leaves off a bough, and ready itself for the next arrivals. No one came to Trippi thinking to level ground, raise timber, and if any lingered, it was with the knowledge that the stay was temporary, a stepping stone to someplace else.

On their last day in Trippi, they visited the Antonin Monument. Made of greenish bronze, it was set inside a filigree fence whose gate was permanently kept open. A series of steps had been carved into its marble pedestal, comfortably worn for sitting or sleeping. Obligingly, Freddie and Manx placed their hands at Antonin's feet to claim its healing; Kish and Renu refused.

"He probably received that treatment from islanders all

his life," said Kish, who after all had been raised by a revolutionary.

Renu shrugged. She had made a decision to keep away from any supernatural phenomena.

They were to head back home that afternoon, and Renu felt herself growing heavy-hearted at the idea. She didn't want to retrace their steps just yet, and longed to go elsewhere. As a child, she'd never liked journeys to end. On car rides, she so enjoyed herself as the yellow highway lines flew by and her thoughts raced with one another that she was always disappointed when the car would stop. Her parents would turn around to find an angry young girl. Grudgingly, she'd climb out, secretly vowing never to be deluded again that things could last.

"You know, Cosu is only two hours from here, yet I've never come to Trippi before," said Kish.

"It is?"

"We can't go there," he said at once. "I skipped out on my exams and everything. Amir would kill me."

"You don't have to see him. We could just sort of sneak in and sneak out."

"It's a very small town; anyway, there's nothing to see there."

"He would probably be thrilled to see you and happy to meet us."

"Yes, I guess he's forgiven me by now. I don't know. It's not like I did it to hurt him, and I can't help thinking that he would have done the same thing. I can't imagine myself in school again—god." Kish sighed. "Do you know the story about the golden mango? The one where Shiva and Parvati promise a mango to whoever could go around the world the fastest?"

He told her the story. Once, the god-parents offered this contest to their god-offspring. Murugan, the firstborn, immediately reined his peacock to his chariot and flew around the earth. But Ganesha, the second son, the elephant-headed god, cupped his palms together and paced a path around his radiant parents. "You are my world," he told them, winning the prize.

"I mean, I can't always be Ganesha," said Kish. "We're all raised with that expectation, that if we're good to our parents, we'll do well in the world. I want to do good by Amir, but I want to see the world outside him, too."

"You can leave again," said Renu.

The others were enthusiastic about the plan and they set off for Cosu at once.

They passed the bazaar on their way to the bus stop. Only Manx had ears for the vendors who called out their wares. She stopped to buy a horoscope scroll.

"Let me read you what it says," she said.

"I can't believe you bought that," said Renu.

"They're all different!"

The girls began to argue as they walked. Enwrapped in their dispute, they didn't notice that Freddie and Kish had stopped at another booth. They were watching a pair of men demonstrate some product. Speaking rapidly, almost songlike, one man swiftly rubbed a brown substance on the bald head of another man, who was seated in a chair. Still speaking, the first man wiped his hands and then spread them apart like a ringmaster.

The crowd watched the seated man. A few laughs filtered through the onlookers and several people began to edge away, when there was a shout. The man began to grow hair! First his bare pate began to fill with a slight fuzz, which darkened and grew bushy. Even as the onlookers drew their breaths, the man had a sizable head of hair, tickling his ears, reaching down his neck.

"Vitagrowth!" shouted the first man. "Vitagrowth!" he

proclaimed, raising his hands in victory over a stunned and respectful crowd.

And instantly the crowd surged forward, tiny bottles were exchanged for rupee notes, promises and miracles were tossed from the man's mouth, and if a bottle slipped and fell to the ground, releasing a trickle of gooey liquid, no one minded, and another was hastily given.

Thus it came about that the four travelers found themselves with a couple of bottles of hair-growth oil while waiting for the bus to Cosu.

"Well, all right, go ahead and try," said Freddie, squatting down in front of Kish.

Kish carefully dabbed some of the brown mixture on a bald portion of Freddie's scalp. Three sets of eyes eagerly awaited the results of the miracle potion. Minutes passed. Fifteen, twenty slowly eased by.

"Nothing's happening."

"It feels a little ticklish."

"Maybe it takes longer."

"Maybe you ought to put more on—I don't think you put enough on."

"It's really tickly."

"I'm sure that guy put more on."

"I don't want any more chemicals seeping through my scalp."

"Maybe you should rub it around a little."

"Are there instructions on the bottle?"

"You mean you didn't read the instructions?"

"Wait—I think I see something—"

"Where? Where?"

"It's only a shadow."

"I think we've been had."

"You think it's a gyp?"

"I think I'll get a rash."

"I don't get it."
"It doesn't work."

The bus wasn't crowded and they found seats together. Round houses shaped out of reed and grass sat like Buddhas on stilts at the edge of Cosu, and further on, a large village guardian stood, its brightly painted sword raised high, its mustaches as glossy black as a matinee idol's. This was Aburanger, semilateral descendant of the Sphinx, an ancient demigod, protector of reed-dwellers, farmers, merchants, banisher of evil. Somewhere along the line, however, Aburanger had been transformed from a rural deity into a superstar, his statues getting bigger and more decorated. He became a god for the bankers, for computer-builders and stockholders. His original followers, the Banacs, felt he'd betrayed them, and turned their attention elsewhere.

The Banacs were the first inhabitants of Pi. They were a fierce, nomadic people who had slashed and burned their way through the forests, and had then been pushed into the interior by the waves of Mogul and Indian invaders. By the time of the British, who had little use for tribes, the Banacs were considered an antediluvian threat to colonialism, and a long, half-hearted war ensued. Eventually, discouraged by an enemy who so constantly eluded them, the British sent a peace delegation to the tribal leaders to negotiate a treaty. The delegation had not been gone long when its members were discovered dead; the circumstances of the deaths were mysterious, but public reaction was not. European newspapers picked up the story of Caliban-descendants, tree monsters who ate their wives and babies, and funds were solicited for troops versed in jungle fighting. Organizations in St. James's Square knitted socks for the soldiers, and two or three men claimed to have escaped from the very stewpots, as it were, and lived to tell the tale. The slaughter of the Banac tribe was swift and merciless.

Renu looked upon the land, which gave no sign of its former inhabitants, a people whose god had been abducted and remade. If she were in Delhi, she could see their prayer bowls, their body ornaments, even a reconstructed cooking site in a museum. But the island had lost them, the purposely homeless had been denied wandering ground. The island had been occupied so many times, no one held any real claims. Even she had no birthright, and by leaving once, had become as foreign as any invader.

Eighteen

She'd never seen so many umbrellas. Hundreds of them jostled with one another, brilliantly colored and blooming like flowers. Renu felt as if she'd landed in a secret garden.

Konga was sitting in the front of the shop, picking his teeth with a thin stick.

"So you've come back," he said, stick between his teeth.

Kish nodded. He felt as if he'd entered a diorama, a world in miniature; yet he felt excited, the way one does viewing something familiar after a long absence. Everything was lit with potential. Giddy with the aftereffects of travel, Kish found his tongue at last.

"Yes, I've been away." He paused. Then he rapidly plunged into introductions, proud of his new friends, emboldened by the obvious fact that old Konga was the same insect as ever, while *he* had undergone tremendous change. Konga—damn him!—acknowledged the others by the slightest inclination of his head, running his tongue over his gums.

"Where's Amir?" asked Kish.

"Resting." Konga indicated with his head. "Inside. He's been lying there for weeks. It's probably nothing, it's not getting any worse. Maybe he's sick. Who can say?" Konga spat near their feet. "He thinks he's dying."

Everything drained out of Kish, the streams of newly acquired experience leaving him like strands of air. Nothing in life was easy.

"Don't stand there like an idiot, boy—go in and see him."

They were left with Konga. It was a mistake to come, thought Renu, sinking inside herself, wishing they were all back on the bus again. It was a mistake, it was wrong, they should not have come.

Manx wandered around the umbrellas, marveling.

Konga was silent, hunkered on his haunches. Gaunt and edgy. Freddie studied him, this legend, this cowboy infiltrator, silent radical. What must he feel, his cause having come to naught, his life little improved? Was he still a believer in his ideals, or had he left them aside as less urgency accompanied his actions? What did a former island revolutionary think about?

Manx startled him out of his reverie. Breathless from her tour around the yard, she immediately addressed Konga: "Did you ever kill anyone?"

"Well, did you find it?"
   "Almost."
   "Oh?"
   "A fake."
   "There are swindlers and thieves all over."
   "I was in jail."
   "Consider it experience."
   "Adda Krishnamurthi set me free."
   "It is his life's calling."
   Kish looked at Amir lying on the bed-mat, propped up on one elbow and listening. He didn't look good, tiredness replacing vigor, a weakness softening all his hard lines. Kish stood stiffly in his adopted father's presence, willing himself not to be affected by the way Amir looked.

"I can't stay."

"I know."

In a minute he was on his knees, sobbing on Amir's chest, shaking with remorse.

"My boy, my boy," crooned Amir, holding him the way he used to hold him as a child.

Konga didn't answer Manx immediately. He didn't know the numbers. There were those who'd been killed in raids or bombings, accidents he'd set up, the army and police corps that the party regularly fought, civilians caught in the cross-fire. The first two had been army kids, not yet sixteen; he'd stumbled over them later in the dark. After that, it ceased to matter, and the killings became part of an eternal falling, a process that, once begun, kept on going of its own will and had no real connection to him. When Konga stopped dream-ing of those two boys, he began to wait for a click, a moment of some kind that would signal *something*. Not spiritual, for he spit on the gods, but possibly existential, a reconciliation in himself, a settling of sand. This vague anticipation was sublimated by his sliding into the life that followed the party's disbanding, but not entirely eliminated. Konga was still wait-ing and it made him nervous all the time.

"Hundreds," he said finally.

"Are his nieces outside?"

"Yes."

"Call them in."

When they entered the room, Amir was trying to get out of bed, restrained only by Kish. If Adda was tall and thin enough to be blown away by the wind, Amir was squat and solidly attached to the earth. Wearing a striped T-shirt that only emphasized his roundness, he reminded Renu of the high school coach.

"I am Amir."

"Yes."

"We used to call your mother stumble-legs. She could never walk three steps without tripping. Adda used to hoist her on his shoulders when he'd have to watch her. 'But Amma, Amir and I want to play,' he'd say, and your grandmother would yell, '*Array*, she's just a baby, you won't even notice her.' What a crier she was—we used to feed her mango ice cream all the time."

"Did he never tell you the story of how he was sent to market to purchase a cow, and came back with two wild boars, because he'd heard that the Swiss health spas were bottling boar's milk?"

"Once, he convinced the entire second form that it was Queen Victoria's birthday and sent them home thinking it was a holiday. What a thrashing he received for that! Your grandfather came to school and gave him a second beating in front of the schoolmaster, and damned if Adda didn't take the scale out of his father's hand and break it in two! They stood fuming at one another until the schoolmaster, at his wit's end, declared it a holiday after all, and dismissed us again."

"Your grandfather of course had no use for me. He was such a proper man, and thought I was a loafer, a bad influence. 'Are you going to sleep your entire lives away?' he'd ask when he'd find us lying about in the grass. 'We're discovering planets,' your uncle would say."

"We used to watch motion pictures. We'd climb over the compound wall of the Britishmen's Club, sneak across the lawn, go up the trellis, and from a window, where we could make ourselves a seat, we'd see lots of films. We'd see Charlie Chaplin, Buster Keaton, Mabel Normand, Rod La Rocque, all the old movies they'd recycle from abroad. We mugged up *The Mark of Zorro* and acted it out together."

"Adda never told you this? How can you not know this? It is your legacy."

"Your grandfather as I said had no use for me, but when Adda went away, he came to see me and gave me his letters. Write to him, he told me, for he wanted his son back, even if only to return and fight for the island. It was all beginning then. By the time Adda returned from Europe, I'd already met the Wasp and was deeply committed."

"At first, he wanted no part of the war—he wanted to write poetry. So we'd hold our meetings, and all of our men would be swearing and drinking, ready to spill blood despite Gandhi, and Adda would be off in a corner, writing love verses to his wife."

"Finally, he got interested, when he realized he'd come back to the same home, that nothing had changed, his father was only an older version of the father he'd left, his mother was still the same. So he became a real member of our party— intelligence officer, we made him, for the fellow's a genius. He left Nirmila Nivasam and lived with me, and his wife came, too."

Amir told this story late into the night. But he was selective with his memory, choosing his details deliberately. He did not speak of the schism that drove the two friends apart. He did not speak of how, after Independence, Adda went to Delhi to sit in Congress, or how Alphonsa, daily finding life more and more unbearable, turned religious. He did not speak of himself, of why after Adda's departure, he became more and more reckless, taking part in death-wish raids and attacks, until he finally landed in jail. He told them what they already knew: that Adda returned to the island to find his life rent asunder. His wife was in a convent, his best friend in jail, and neither would send for him.

Nineteen

My boy is back and my strength returns," declared Amir from his bed, and indeed, there was a quickness about his movements that hadn't been there before. Kish and Freddie had been dispatched to the Agra Hotel, from which they brought back soft rice cakes, an array of chutneys and savories, all wrapped ready to go in plantain leaves and string. They sat down to eat around Amir's bed, while he watched with the delighted repose of a round-bellied Deccan sultan.

"See, I still have the vigor of an ox," said Amir, holding high his cup of coconut wine.

Freddie lit up and passed his joint to Amir but Amir waved it away, explaining he never smoked ganja, that it affected his heart.

"But what a strong lion of a heart I have, eh, Konga?"

"You have a greasy, tiny heart," said Konga.

"I have a strong, sound heart," roared Amir.

The door was open and people began to wander in. They came to greet Kish, have a look at the strangers, sitting on the floor, on the windowsills, and at the doorway. They said hello to neighbors they hadn't seen for a day, offered snatches of radio-news and gossip, brought in more food and drink. A space was cleared and tablas were brought out; two drummers, joined by a guitarist, began to play sweetly and severely. The music began softly, then built to an incessant rhythm that at first burst thrumming in the ears, then bent itself inside out with an interplay of liquid strumming and drumbeats, until the sounds flowed like a river, washing gently from the ears to the fingers and toes and there was no division, no separation, no distinction, just music, just sound.

Long ago, Renu and Rajesh had tried to teach themselves guitar. She didn't remember where the instrument had come from. It was a tiny thing with fading green and red stripes, someone's initials scratched out on the back. They had sheets of chords, tiny diagrams showing finger placement on the frets. They thought they could play by humming the melody and stroking the strings. Renu remembered how they fought over the instrument, determined to best one another. Why were they such contenders? Proudly they showed off their first calluses, but their playing remained awful. Neither of them, to Chitra's disgust, had the patience to concentrate. She tried to teach them a little, and in the end, began to play more often than they did. But she abandoned it as well, finding it lacked what she had in the veena and violin.

They were singing now. Amir leaned on Kish, hugging his back. Their easy intimacy both embarrassed and fascinated Renu—to be held like that, so securely and completely, without squirming. The men in her family were not huggers; awkwardly, they'd pat a shoulder, and if overcome with emotion, grab a portion of the body, the head, say, squeeze briefly and let go, both participants relieved the exhibition was over. Kish looked like he could spend a life in Amir's arms.

. . .

Where were Freddie and Manx?

She wandered outside, around the village square. Awnings were rolled up, metal lattice gates pulled shut until morning when the shopkeepers would clang them back, sweep water on the doorsteps to settle the dust, and resume business. No one was about, everyone was at Amir's, the quiet unnatural. It was with some relief that Renu saw Konga sitting against a tree, blowing out blue smoke from a cigarette.

"Why aren't you celebrating with the others?" he asked as she approached.

She shrugged; she might have asked the same of him. She didn't know whether to sit down or not, and as she could get no hint from him whether he wanted company or solitude, she drew a breath and took the plunge.

"When are you leaving?" he asked as soon as she was seated.

Renu merely looked at him.

"When are you going back to Madhupur?" he asked.

"I don't know," she said.

Konga was silent, and if Renu had cared she would have been uncomfortable. But the funny thing was she no longer cared what impression she might be making, merely sat through it all, absent.

"No good will come of any of this," he said.

Renu watched a tiny red ant crawl along the dirt and onto her foot.

"For twenty years my general and I have had coffee every morning, and we have said good night to each other every evening. Some things should be left alone."

Renu hardly felt the ant bite.

"For twenty years, the pestilence has been fading. You don't know what pestilence is like. You don't know what it is like to be haunted for what seems an eternity, to be so tormented by your memory that you want to bore a hole into your head. There are terrible, terrible things to twist a man's soul, and you are too much a baby to know any of it—"

"I know something of it," said Renu.

"What would you know? You maybe have seen a tragic movie once—no, you know nothing of it."

Another ant headed her way.

"Your coming is no good. Amir has been trying to rid himself of the curse of your family for years."

"But he seems very happy to see us," said Renu.

"Yes, it will start up all over again. You come here with the boy, you return to Madhupur, you tell your uncle about your visit, memories are reopened, the past is reconsidered, events are retraced, re-enacted, remembering will blur the pain, but the pain," and here Konga looked at Renu with a terrible face, "the pain can never be escaped. It will seem fine and pretty in the beginning, but the wounds will slowly reopen—"

"I don't know what you're talking about."

"Amir should not return to Adda. The past should rest," said Konga.

"Do you mean they shouldn't see one another?" asked Renu. Konga was silent. "Why shouldn't they see each other?" asked Renu in exasperation.

"Because my general was in love with your uncle's wife, the Spanish slut."

"My aunt?"

Konga looked at Renu to see the effect of his words but, finding only bafflement, he looked away. The cicadas began their electric concert, droning from one tree to the next, invisible noisemakers. Addressing them instead of Renu, who was now wary, not certain she wanted to hear any of this, he began his story.

"My general is a strange man. Never had he so much as looked at a woman before the Spanish. The island was his love, and he wanted to protect her, determined to save her from the rape of the white man. After Independence, India wanted to draw us to her, and the National Congress offered us representation. Adda was among those who thought we should accept their invitation, while Amir was bitterly opposed to the idea. India was an indifferent mother, feeding us on whim, abandoning us when it came to our own battles, and to accept this offer was to lose ourselves. We are not India, we are not Sri Lanka, we are not Hong Kong. But Adda, fattened on European bread, stupid as a scholar, thought we should at least explore the possibility.

"I remember the day he left, garlanded like a movie star at the pier, all of us waving and shouting luck. If nothing else, we shouted, bring back the newspapers. That was our joke, of course, the island so cut off from everything else. His sisters were all huddled together, crying, because the last time he left the island, he didn't return for ten years. The Spanish stood by herself. There was never any question of her going."

"What happened with my aunt and Amir?" asked Renu, but Konga did not appear to hear her.

"Everyone thought she went to the convent for Jesus, but she just went to hide her belly."

"She was pregnant?"

"She went away, and it was only the two of us, Amir and me, but Amir began to go crazy. He started his stunts, planning madman attacks on the temporary Ministry office, wanting to set all the trees on fire so American planes could see our strength, live in the forests like holy men one minute, in the caves like panthers the next. Our men left us, what could they do? He finally landed in jail, only that fool Adda bailed him out."

Konga's words trailed away; he had slipped back into the past. With effort, Renu spoke.

"What happened with my aunt?"

Konga seemed startled to find her still there.

"What happened? The Spanish died, the baby lived," he said absently.

"Who was the father?" asked Renu slowly, straining with impatience, trying to keep calm.

Konga looked at her curiously.

"Adda," he replied.

"Adda?"

"Of course Adda," he replied with annoyance.

"I don't understand," said Renu, confused. What had she missed?

Konga took a breath, lit another cigarette, and began again.

"That was what she told me in that bare cell with the picture of the Christian goddess on the wall. 'I am going to die,' she said. 'Adda is the father but the child should go to Amir.' She stood there holding her belly as if it were a gift, and I, wretch that I was, so taken with the way she looked, trying to be brave and beyond pity, resolute as a saint, I agreed. Her announcement of death came as no surprise, I didn't care what happened to her. I didn't question her, I thought it was something she knew, that it was the truth. But I agreed to the other, I couldn't *not* agree, do you understand? I only said, give him time, let him stay in jail and calm down. She understood. Amir was not rational then, you don't get to be the Number One Enemy of Pi by being rational.

"But Adda came back and got Amir out. I was the one who took him to Cosu, I told him Banac land was perfect for subversive action. I thought that in the confusion over her suicide—for it had to be that—the baby would be lost, it would die, I don't know what I thought. But the nuns tracked us down, they brought him the boy."

"The boy?" asked Renu, beginning to understand at last.

Konga merely snorted. Renu felt a spasm of pain. Looking down, she saw several ants crowded on her foot, biting fiercely. With a cry of alarm, she jumped up, frantically brushing them off, shuddering. Konga watched impassively.

"Why didn't you tell him?" she asked, looking straight at him.

"Tell who?"

"Anyone. Kish could have grown up at Nirmila Nivasam, he could have—" but Renu stopped as the impact of the revelation hit.

Now Konga looked straight back at her. "And take away the one thing Amir had? Independence was won but left him nothing. He could not love his friend, he could not love the Spanish. Take from Amir the one thing he could love freely? The boy helped heal Amir. Why, you've never heard a man scream the way Amir could scream. He'd start drinking the moment he woke up, go to bed with liquor dripping from his lip. He would bat at his face, trying to shake the memory, the anguish. He'd cry out in the night, thrashing, unnerved, my god, so crazed."

"But what about Kish?"

"The boy didn't suffer. He grew up with a man who was his father by choice, devoted by choice. Do you know how rare that is? Why, my father used to beat me every morning, because he said it woke up his hand. Kish never suffered."

"But it's wrong to know something like that and not tell."

"Well, I've told you." Konga's voice grew softer. "The thing is you can't protect anyone. I thought the farther Amir was from Adda, the better, and I still believe it. But Kish went ahead and found Adda anyway. Amir gave Kish all his love and the boy just ran away from him. That's the way it is with people. You give your heart completely to anything and it turns on you—"

"No—"

"The past will always return to drag you back to the river."

"No."

"Why do you keep saying no? My general is an old man, Adda is an old man, and life is nothing more than a march toward death."

"But isn't it horrible that people die without knowing the truth?"

"People die anyway."

"It's not right."

"Look, I do not care to make judgments anymore on what's right and wrong. I've told you the truth, as you so call it. Do with it what you will."

And with those words, Konga left her.

Twenty

Kish her cousin. It seemed impossible. Renu could only re-
peat the idea aloud to test its strangeness but it remained
no less amazing. Her mysterious aunt!

Alphonsa in her cumbersome caftan, Alphonsa with her
hesitant eyes, a woman growing more and more uneasy with
her life on the island. Hadn't she left Cádiz for something
different, a taste of the exotic, a promise of adventure? Only
to discover that tradition wove as tight a weave around its
islanders as it did in Spain, that things weren't as she imagined
them to be. She was shunned and left alone, not allowed to
sit with Adda as he ate his meals with the other men, and
not able to eat in ease with the women. Renu thought of her
aunt on stifling summer nights, unable to find relief from the
heat, the mosquitoes, the heavy air. For somewhere in there—
it *had* to be so—Adda no longer offered her shade, could not
help ease her burden as she plowed through her days.

She wondered how Amir must have appeared to her bored
and lonely aunt. Had she always harbored a secret crush on
her husband's friend, or had Amir's attraction been revealed
to her slowly, after years of talking, translating, walking with
him? Had accidental fingertip brushes been followed by

blushes, confusion, painful silence for days afterwards, or had they merely turned to each other in sexy expectation one afternoon? Amir must have been a romantic highwayman, a rough-and-ready revolutionary, a gold-hearted bandit to break through her mathematical order, her geometrically planned world.

Amir arriving one day for translation at her tidy bungalow. Alphonsa parting the gossamer curtain in the doorway of her bedroom where she'd been arranging flowers. Amir waiting seated in the cane chair, sweating from the heat in his sleeve-less undershirt. Alphonsa lifting her arms to fix a bloom in her hair, pausing on the threshold. From this, everything.

Adda was the center, the missing crux in the untold story between Konga's words and what she already knew. Adda must have never been far from their thoughts, and it was the idea of Adda that must have surely led them on. If they had gone to him with the truth, would he have blessed them like a saint? Or would he have been the one to go crazy? Useless speculation. Alphonsa died, Amir went crazy, and Adda was left mystified. Leave the past alone, and it will not trouble you, Aunt Bala would say. A body of literature backed her up; dig into the past and only murder and incest will result, it proved over and over again.

But Renu had been born with questions in her mouth, disregarding precedent. Konga had given her the burden of truth, and what was she supposed to do with it? Bend to adapt, her aunt would say, a woman whose back sometimes bent parallel to the ground.

The sun was setting, orange and purple clouds snaking the sky. She began to walk toward the beach. Her stomach was churning and she felt hot all over. If she could just get calm for a while, step away from the anxiety to help her rationality back to shape, she believed she could handle it. But no matter how she tried to clear her mind, Kish came up all over. She crossed the darkening sand, the square far behind her. What would Rajesh do? Unfailingly, her mind slipped back into the tread it knew best. What would her cousin do? Renu began to imagine what he might say, wanting fiercely the innocence they had as children, when everything was an adventure, when they could clasp their hands and with two heads, solve any problem put forth to them. This was what she longed for, her old companion who so easily and constantly relieved the possibility of doing anything by herself.

Her mind was crowding up. There were too many thoughts at once.

I didn't want him to die
I don't know what to do
I hate being alone
What else?

She stumbled and picked her way along the water wet with moon. Her feet tripped over driftwood, an empty bottle smoothed by sand, encrusted with shells. Tiny cowries lay hidden like turtles, small as the ones she and Rajesh used to collect for games of Parcheesi.

Why did it have to be him? How come it was him and not me? How come it was me who went to America and he who had to die? If he'd gone to America, maybe he'd have liked it better. He could have joined the track team, signed up for Debating. He would have had more fun. It would have been different if he'd been there too. We would have all been different. And how come I couldn't see the funeral? I wanted to know whether the body was placed in a sack, or whether they tossed him as he was. Is it so horrible to want to know details? I want to know everything. But even if we had made it on time, they probably would not have let me see. What did they say, that it is lucky I'm protected from that sort of thing. What were they trying to protect me from? All those years, being careful and watching out, locking doors and closing windows, as if there was something out there waiting to get us. Not going anywhere, not doing anything, sitting around while everyone else did everything. Would it have been so horrible if I'd gone to the prom? Did they really think I'd come home pregnant? Manx isn't like that, she does anything she wants, and I'm there clearing her path, and she doesn't even realize it. But if Rajesh had been there, it would have been different. He'd have gone out and done things, he wouldn't have stayed home. It's not fair. I spent all that time doing nothing, and then he dies, and I have to do nothing all over again, because everyone wants it to be me who died, not him. But he didn't go through half of what I went through, the bus rides to school, being called a brownie, the assemblies, gym class. He had Uncle Adda and Aunt Bala and a million other people to turn to, like everyone else had their grandmas in Brooklyn, and they could go into the city to have brunch, and Rajesh was here eating mangoes, all those mangoes. I can't believe they didn't let me see the funeral.

When had it gotten so dark? Somehow she'd left the sea and—no, the sea was still there, weirdly white as if lit from within. Was it Yama who walked toward her, bearing searchlights? Or was Death as certain of his step as a blind man, a map of the world behind his eyelids? Something was bright, something was luminous, something lurid. She was magnet-drawn to it, her body heavy, clay, cement. She thought of weighty blooms that hung to the ground, ready to drop. Nefertiti's neck, someone had used that analogy, some teacher had said that the limestone head and banded toque was like a heavy flower about to topple off a slender stem.

It was an oil drum. Someone had abandoned an oil drum lit with fire on the beach. A hot-chestnut seller in all probability. It gleamed, hot-embered fire, smoky and rancid. Renu took a stick and poked at it, adding her breath to stir it up. She fanned it with her fingers.

Nefertiti—why had she been studying her anyway? What was the point of all that information, all the reading, all the studying? Rajesh was smarter, hadn't that always been the case? Why wasn't she more like her sister, going her own way, doing what she pleased? Her sister's head must be light as a balloon released—oh, she'd gotten too close, she'd burned her finger. It didn't hurt. It didn't hurt at all. Woozy, she held up her finger to see the blister, the scar, some sign, but there was none. Maybe, thought Renu dully, maybe she'd discovered something. Another secret.

Sati. The fire looked beautiful now, the flames leaping up, the smoke almost fragrant. The coals in the drum burned orange, smoldering red, a sun contained by rusty metal. Guilt by association, trial by fire, a test of loyalty witnessed by the gods. Didn't King Rama demand that his wife, the lotus-born, step into the fire to prove her chastity? Sita, Uma, Brunhild, all brides of fire, of faith. *The nymphs are departed.* Who said that? The coals burned and she smelled the fishy fire. Rats ran down into the water, scampering across the river's dead. The river ran into the sea, the sea ran away, who stood alone? Rajesh was seated in the fire, holding out a hand, brown and thin like hers, hand to hand the circle complete, and then she'd find rest.

The fire called her name, her true name. Manx had a made-up name to ward off the family. Meenakshi might have to acknowledge the foreignness, the rules that made her life different from the milkstream of her American friends. But Manx invented her own image and disclaimed biography, while Renu was all too ready to claim her past, join the line of Krishnan women who lowered their gaze and trusted in the families chosen for them. Renu thought she was different, she had a twin, a secret thread that connected her to a world only the two shared, that made them separate from their mothers, their uncles. It was like knowing a secret language.

But she'd relied too much on Rajesh, because he was smarter, he was the boy, the favored child within their twinness.

The fire called and she crouched to coat her palms with sand. The grains slid off easily, and she embraced the warm metal of the drum. It was like heat fomentation. She remembered her mother sitting by the oven, and pressing a warm cloth to her throat when she had the flu. The flames were vivid, hot, and she was inside their combustion. Heat gave way to cool blue, layers of water, layers of heaven. Someone was singing. Who was singing?

They appeared, three women, three familiar women carrying stones. Their muscles rippled as they lifted the stones above their heads, and then it was the Seer, opening her wings and flying with her mystery soothsaying, her herbal potions, and she took off her dark glasses and became Mirazi, a necklace of stones around her slender neck. Alphonsa appeared next, radiant in her pregnancy, her belly round and smooth as a stone. They appeared before her, pulling stones out of their pockets, letting them fall from their hair. To dream of stones is to dream of numberless perplexities, to dream of pebbles is to dream of faults.

Choose your light, they said, opening their arms like Demeter welcoming Persephone home. And Renu, in a half-awake, half-asleep state, looked from the fire to their arms. The light made her squint, her eyes were so tired. *Renu*, called Rajesh. She turned back to the fire and willed herself nearer—it would be easy and quick, but just as she was about to crawl inside, something made her stop. Something awakened in her and shot to her head, and with a gasp, she fell away from the fire.

Rajesh was dead but she was alive! That was it, the essence, the absurdity, the tragedy, the truth. Her stomach heaved and she threw up. Then she began to cry.

. . .

When Kish found her, she was lying face down on the sand. He shook her awake, and when she turned her blinking eyes and sour breath to him, he sighed with relief. Her hair was singed, an aureole of white framing her face. She looked like she had returned from the dead.

III

Twenty-one

The island constantly battled artists. Nature seemed indifferent as man constructed out of the elements around him
and the dreams within, stood passive as passion and strength
erected the structure, the sculpture, the object made for no
other reason than to release heartflight. But when everything
was done, champagne opened and spilling on the ground,
when no one was paying attention, nature would remember.
A teasing breeze would rise, build to a tempest that in hours
would destroy all new creation, a sandstorm would brew to
fill all crevices artfully made, the sun would send scorching
heat to peel and cripple paint. Despite this, or because of it,
the island flourished with artists.

The Nigerian was as determined as the rest, and the fact
that his ash pile had been eaten so ferociously by the island
did not dissuade him from building the bridge. The islanders
were behind his efforts, hopeful as he to see the completion,
and mindful, too, of the money to be made from the media
coverage. A festival was to be held at the shore, a night-long
affair to celebrate the bridge. While the artist toiled on his
vision, shopkeepers swept their steps in anticipation of crowds
and city officials had their shoes shined. Cartons of fireworks,

the kind that spiraled and snaked, arrived and tables were built to accommodate the food and visitors, and a podium was set up for speeches. Dignitaries from Sri Lanka and India as well as some European movie stars were expected. An orphan's choir was engaged. It was to be a grand event.

"There's no reason why you should not see it. The newspapers say it is an event of historic proportions."

"Nothing but cheap publicity. What's the point of connecting Pi to the mainland?"

"It's symbolic. Anyway, you'll be the only one not there."

"It will be a day to count the fools in town."

"It will be a good day for you to get out."

"I've *been* out. And you can close the shutter now, I've had enough air."

But Bala ignored her father's request and remained seated on the veranda, her chair pulled up near the window of his room. She snapped beans in her lap, separating what would be used and what wouldn't into two piles. She hadn't really thought he'd changed his mind, but she feared his legs were atrophying. And he was probably killing his heart as well, she thought, reminding herself to ask Adda about it. Her brother was at Srinath Station, waiting for their nieces and their friends to return. They'd received a cable yesterday, a week after Rukmani and Chitra returned from *their* trip.

She could hear her sisters giggle from somewhere in the house. What silly creatures they were! Ever since their return, they'd been closeted in one room or another, speaking in whispers, and exchanging private glances. Ridiculous creatures!

It would be nice to hear youthful voices again in the house. She liked having the family fill up the rooms, and could not understand the loneliness of American life, with everyone living in a condo and eating out of single-serve soup cans, such a disposable way of living. Better for her nieces to remain here, she thought; they had friends, they had the family. Why, Renu could even marry Kish, it might be a good match. His background was dubious, but there was something so winning about the boy, she'd felt it from the first. He was well formed, his mind was quick, and why, they could easily send him to Madras or Delhi to finish his studies. Whatever he had learned from the outlaws could be unlearned.

So sat Bala musing, when she heard the commotion at the gate. They were back at last! Bala rose eagerly, holding out her arms to the travelers. But her mouth hung open in disbelief; there in front of her stood Highway Amir, Ex-Revolutionary, Number One Enemy of Pi.

Twenty=two

Kish, I have to talk with you," said Renu. She had not been able to talk with him any sooner. "I've got some news."

Quickly, she told him what Konga had told her. After she finished, Kish didn't say anything.

"Well?" she asked.

"I knew already," he said.

Renu was taken aback. "You *knew*? How could you know?"

"I've known for a while. It's not that hard to figure out."

"You knew and didn't say anything? Kish, we're related, we're *cousins* now. Doesn't that make a difference to you?"

Kish shrugged. "We act like family already, don't we? I figured I had a foreign mother, and when I heard about Alphonsa, I put it together. I mean, the woman who took me to Amir knew what she was doing."

"I can't believe it doesn't make a difference that Uncle Adda is your real father."

"I care. But I'm nineteen years old, Renu. I don't want to walk around either Amir or Adda."

. . .

Chitra and Rukmani made much of Renu's return. They showered her with compliments, and eagerly presented her with the results of their hunt. They dropped hints of a medical student in Colombo, a boy whose family was exquisite, and an architect from Kerala who had studied at Stanford. Chitra seemed content, tranquil, and no longer looked at Renu as if she wanted to suck out her breath. She was as intent as Rukmani at getting Renu's future secured.

Renu was astonished that Kish was so casual regarding his parentage. It was so cavalier, and it didn't make much sense. She sighed. She felt so old, like a woman who had lived a full life, a Victorian life. Life seemed to be speeding along, and she with it. Renu took a deep breath. She began to make a list:

1. New clothes
2. New shoes
3. Haircut
4. Choose a major

"What are you reading?"

Freddie put down his book to answer Renu. He showed her the title of the book, one about Sufis and mystics.

"Is it any good? Does it tell you things you can use?"

"It tells you what other people have used. It's a lot of biographies."

"You read a lot of these kinds of books, right?"

"I'm interested, yes."

"Do they give you guidance?"

"Not so much guidance as a presentation of a variety of thought. I mean, we all have this *choice* before us, different ways of perception. I was thinking, it's different from, say, math, where you operate from a base of givens, of absolutes.

From the absolutes, you can prove a theorem about a triangle, but only if you have a given. In our lives, we have no givens, really, and end up groping, trying to stumble upon a truth without knowing the path to follow. If we had a given, it'd be much easier."

"Life and death are givens."

"Right. Life and death and birth and rebirth—it's a cycle, and we can never be sure of where we are exactly."

"Vishnu's Dream?"

"Exactly."

"Do you think that even if we don't know the absolutes, that they still exist?"

"Depends if you believe in a God or not. I mean, we can create absolutes, like a religion, or a type of diet."

Renu nodded. "What are you going to do, Freddie?" she asked.

"I don't know. I heard that Mirazi is in Lahore. I've never been to Pakistan."

"So you're just going to follow her around?"

"At some point, we all have to create an absolute."

Renu made another list:

1. They killed the monkey with the arrow.
2. The monkey was divine and chose to be shot.
3. The arrow's flight and the monkey's fall had nothing to do with one another.

And it occurred to Renu that she'd never know the truth. There was no given in this case. No matter how long she thought about it, she would never know for sure. It wasn't a matter of cause and effect. She stared at the paper as if she'd written her own destiny.

Twenty = three

I'm selling the house, Renu."

When her mother said this, seated in the cane peacock chair like a queen, her arms resting serenely on the chair's arms, Renu wasn't surprised. It was difficult to imagine her mother back on Long Island, in their old house.

". . . and I'm writing to the Simlas. They'll take care of the preliminary work, contact the realtors."

"Good," said Renu, "I can help, too."

Her mother seemed not to hear her and went on speaking of market values and property improvements.

"I can show the house myself, Mom," said Renu quietly. "I'm going back."

The remark surprised them both.

"Will you ever go back?" Grandfather Das asked Freddie.

"To the States? Not likely. I'm looking into Lahore."

"Well, you'll soon realize that there's nothing different out there, it's all the same."

Freddie shook his head. He and Manx had been trying to convince Das to come to the festival, but to no avail.

"What's the point?" he asked. "The island will become so crowded, all those extra people arriving. Thank God we don't have an airport. Can you imagine the traffic congestion? I hear all you need is one airport, and any place becomes a zoo."

"But it will be such an adventure for you," said Manx.

"No, thank you. I'll stay here, if only to balance the land and keep it from tipping into the ocean."

Bala sighed. Her chance of seeing the festival was tied with his decision, and glumly, she resigned herself to her duty.

"Don't think it can't happen," he was saying. "It's happened before in the world, and it will happen again. One moment you have a bit of firm ground under your feet, and the next minute, you'll notice your ankles being splashed, then it's your legs, and suddenly you're covered in water, and everything you know will drown with you. There's no saving it from sinking."

"What about Renu?" asked Freddie.

"She'll meet us there. I know she will," replied Manx.

"You're leaving?" her mother asked for the fifth time. Renu nodded, looking out the window at the coming dusk. "But this is your home, Renu."

And for the fifth time, Renu began all over again, with the mix of patience and annoyance a daughter assumes before a mother when the roles have become blurred and confused, and real compassion is needed, but lacking. Renu told her mother reasons as she made them up, as the dark outside descended and her mother began to rock as if in a trance.

"But Meena will be here."

"Her name is Manx."

"And what about Kish?"

"I don't know what his real name is."

The bridge shimmered like a poem over the water. A thousand tiny lights and candles were attached to it, a glittering thread held up by breath. Some parts of it were nothing more than a length of rope, while other parts consisted of elaborate roofing and floors, a patchwork of bridge-making that reached all the way to India.

Adda and Amir and Kish started off early, hoping to catch some of the preparations, and take a look at the new Chief Minister. As Kish wandered ahead of them, Amir grinned.

"He's a fine boy, eh, Adda?"

"A fine boy."

With regret, Manx and Freddie left Grandfather Das and Aunt Bala, promising to bring back some of the festival in their pockets.

Chitra was searching for her sister. The house was nearly empty. The others had all left, and now a rickshaw driver waited for them at the gate, ready to take them there. At last, she came upon Rukmani and Renu.

"Come on, you girls, let's go, you're slow," she said, bursting into the room, her sari rustling, her shawl tucked securely around her shoulders. Rukmani looked at her sister and then at her daughter, who stared blankly at her.

"Yes, I'm ready. Come along, Renu," said Rukmani, holding out her arms to Renu. But Renu declined. Shrugging, Rukmani took hold of her sister's hand instead and, with feet as light as when they were girls, they tripped down the hallway, onto the porch and across the courtyard to the gate, where they lifted their saris delicately and climbed aboard.

Renu followed the rickshaw in her mind. She watched it rattle down the side street, then on the main road along the beach, past the old downtown and fountain, past the grove of coconut trees outside the German glass factory, and the USIS library, and the Annie Besant school, until it stopped by the Gandhi Memorial and its passengers alighted. When she was certain that her mother and her aunt had arrived at the celebration grounds and had had plenty of time to lose themselves in the crowd, Renu stood up.

She found Aunt Bala and her grandfather playing cards.

"Why, I thought you'd already left," exclaimed Bala.

Renu replied that she'd been late in getting ready, but was on her way now. Bala nodded approvingly.

"Enjoy yourself. There are so many things for you to see," she said.

Her grandfather was silent, waiting to place his winning hand on the bed.

Twenty=four

The road was empty and dark. She used a flashlight to find her way, heedless of the piles of dung on the street, the gaping potholes. Everyone must have gone to the celebration, for most of the houses were dark. Moonlight and a few streetlamps guided her to the beach. She held her breath part of the way, willing all the stray dogs and ruffians and loiterers and witches to leave her alone. It was so dark. She almost bumped into an old woman who was sipping from a bottle in a sack. Renu faltered for a moment, but the woman moved on, hardly noticing her. Renu kept walking, and it seemed to her that the three women of her dreams were waving at her, beckoning her on.

Imagine Renu like this, cut off from the inside of herself and aware of the world—a teeming, passionate world—around her. Imagine that with each step, she was walking away from her superstitions and fears, away from her self-wrought sickness, her desire to live in the past. Imagine her stepping away from her inherited weights, demanding flight.

This is our secret dream, our need to break free from the ground on which we half the time drag our feet resentfully, because we have been told that it is important and correct to feel the earth beneath, even while flight is in our hearts. Weightless travel, metaphorical soul soaring, a shedding of swallowed stones, a mobility that can hold the keys of the universe.

Our heroes are those who defy gravity, the gods who live in the clouds, beings who walk on water, those with magic boots and capes. There are some of us forever at our windows, waiting for rescue from the world outside. But even the sages walked on the earth; they gathered staffs and bowls, placed foot after foot further into life, eyes open, palms open.

Renu Krishnan stood on the beach on the island of Pi, ready for her journey.

A NOTE ON THE TYPE

This book was set in a digitized version of Granjon, a type named in compliment to Robert Granjon, a type cutter and printer active, in Antwerp, Lyons, Rome, and Paris, from 1523 to 1590. Granjon, the boldest and most original designer of his time, was one of the first to practice the trade of type founder apart from that of printer.

Linotype Granjon was designed by George W. Jones, who based his drawings on a face used by Claude Garamond (c. 1480–1561) in his beautiful French books. Granjon more closely resembles Garamond's own type than does any of the various modern faces that bear his name.

Composed by PennSet, Inc., Bloomsburg, Pennsylvania
Printed and bound by The Haddon Craftsmen, Inc.,
Scranton, Pennsylvania
Designed by Virginia Tan

10 - 3/20/95